RECOGNITION

RECOGNITION

O.H. BENNETT

BOLDEN

AN **AGATE** IMPRINT

CHICAGO

Printed in the United States of America.

Library of Congress Cataloging-in-Publication Data

Bennett, O. H. (Oscar H.), 1957-

Recognition / O. H. Bennett.

    pages cm

Summary: ""A woman becomes obsessed with finding a homeless man she glimpses on the street, who resembles her husband who disappeared a decade earlier"--Provided by publisher"-- Provided by publisher.

    ISBN 978-1-932841-79-4 (pbk.) -- ISBN 1-932841-79-2 (pbk.)

    1. Husband and wife--Fiction. 2. Missing persons--Fiction. 3. African American families--Fiction. I. Title.

    PS3552.E54747R43 2013

    813'.54--dc23

                    2013020475

10 9 8 7 6 5 4 3 2 1

Bolden is an imprint of Agate Publishing. Agate books are available in bulk at discount prices. For more information go to agatepublishing.com.

For Bigman, Oscar H. Bennett Sr.

I. THE LONG BAD DAY

Sirens still frightened her. In the car, she looked around frantically, over one shoulder, then the other, for the source of the screaming. Someone was having a bad day, and a bad day, Dana knew, could last a long, long time. For nearly a mile, she had not put her foot on the gas, just eased off the brakes and allowed the car to inch forward. Rain fell sporadically, spattering her windshield and hood with hundreds of crystal drops. Though it was early in the evening, the clouds, in a wide palette of gray, made it seem later and added to her impatience. Slashing light and slashing sound cut through her car as another siren surged from behind and the cars in her rear mirror parted. Her heart jumped and she jerked the car to the side, feeling for the road's shoulder, feeling the right-side tires crunch rocks.

The ambulance shook her car as it went by. The wind carried another brief drenching of rain, which ended as abruptly as it had started. She watched the progress of the red strobe light down the highway. The accident appeared to be a good mile or more away. She could see the red flickering against the sky's gray ceiling. The light and the siren and the rain led her back to cracked glass, imperfect cubes of broken windshield in her lap, and the voice of the police officer. *Ma'am? Ma'am? Hold on, we're going to get you out of there.* Dana eased off the brake and let her car roll. She picked up her cell phone to call her son Franklin as she had ten minutes ago, only to discover that she had let the batteries run down, as she had discovered ten minutes ago. She tossed the phone onto the passenger seat, where it bounced and fell to the floor. She hoped he would order pizza or go next door to Brenda's. Dana was getting close to the accident now. The two lanes of southbound traffic were being herded into one. He would do his homework first. Never heard of a kid who wanted to do nothing but school work. At first, Dana was quite proud of him and his grades, but now it seemed he used the schoolwork to hide from people. He could disappear and not get into any trouble because he was doing what he was supposed to be doing, and he could avoid everyone. He participated in no sports, no team activities. He did belong to a couple of after-school clubs that he never spoke of. He swam on Sundays. Just a bookworm, she thought. For some reason, when she thought of the word "bookworm," she pictured her son as he was newly born, pale and bald like larvae. Someone honked at her. She wasn't keeping up with the slow procession.

The minutes passed, matched to the crawl of the traffic. The man in the car next to hers had been eyeing her, but turned his head when she looked his way.

The rain turned furious again. An oasis of light shone where the emergency vehicles had encircled the accident. There was a little black car with its front end completely caved in, its windshield a gap-toothed grin. A pickup truck was on its side. Another crumpled car faced the wrong direction. There was no way to glean what had happened from the current positions of the cars involved. The strobe lights of the emergency vehicles revealed plastic and glass shards scattered everywhere. The back of one ambulance was open and the white insides looked impossibly bright in contrast to the dark evening. Dana could lean to the passenger side and see people working in there. She saw a man pulling a piece of equipment from a shelf and another hand reaching. A woman stood outside the ambulance with her hands covering her face. *Her bad day is just beginning.*

Dana was aware her breathing had quickened. Little cubes of bloody glass. She saw her windshield crumble. The glass was in her lap, small crystals stained red were on her chest like crumbs, as if she had eaten glass. Her wet windshield reflected the light from the ambulance. Someone knocked on her window. *We'll get you out of there, lady.* But this cop, covered in a clear raincoat, tapped her glass with a flashlight; his face was in a snarl. "Hey, move it along before I write you up."

Dana had zoned out. Her face flushed. She mouthed *I'm sorry* to the officer, but risked one more glance. The woman at the back of the ambulance looked to be shouting something. *I'm sorry,* Dana imagined the woman saying.

Despite her headlights, the road was reflective black. The taillights of the car in front were pin sized. The rest of the commute looked to be easy. The trickle of emancipated cars left a lot of maneuvering room and everyone was making up time despite the rain. The traffic congestion didn't return until the businesses flanking the road and the traffic lights in Yorkshire and Manassas Park held them up. Just two miles beyond the accident, the road was perfectly dry and the evening sky was considerably lighter, but bands of clouds were coming in. Ahead was the light to turn left on Liberia Avenue and then it was just three turns and four blocks to home. Traffic had tightened, so it was going to take two, maybe three, rotations of the light to get through the intersection. On the concrete median stood a shambling, shaggy rag of a man. He held up a crumpled cardboard sign. He waited until the light turned red and began walking down the line of his captured audience. Even from her distance, Dana could see people rolling down their windows to hand him change or a dollar or two. She looked at her bag in the passenger seat, but did not reach for it. Why should she enable some alcoholic to continue his addiction? She was a schoolteacher; people should be rolling down windows to hand her money; at least she was trying to earn hers. She thought about school for the next couple of minutes. Then the turn arrow was green again and Dana let her car ease forward. By now she calculated she had been behind the wheel for an hour and twenty minutes. She could feel herself growing tired and cranky the way her kids did when they hadn't gotten enough sleep the night before. She flipped her visor down and looked in the make-up mirror. She told herself she wanted to see if she looked as tired as she felt. Her mind replayed parts of her day, especially when her principal had asked her to take the lead on the science fair. Dana had immediately demurred and Anne's face had hardened. "I need to see my teachers involved in the school community," she had said and walked away. *I'm a single parent*, she should have shouted after her, *what time do I have?*

The light turned red. Dana slowed to a stop and saw she was only eight cars back from the light. She could see the shaggy beggar a little bit better now. He had wild wires of hair sticking cactus-like from his beard and moustache. He was momentarily backlit by the red traffic light and looked as if his head was on fire. His sign read "Need change. Need a chance."

Dana was immediately suspicious. The sign read like ad slogan-eering. Repetition, consonance...fairly nice for a homeless addict. She had always wondered if beggars were authentic or just grifters too lazy or too smart to suffer through nine-to-fives like the rest of us.

He was working his way toward her.

Come on light, turn green. Turn green. She repeated this mantra even as the driver two up from her dropped change into the beggar's opened palm.

The shape in the next car waved him away.

He held up his sign for the driver in front of Dana. That window came down.

Turn green. It turned.

He was handed what looked like two ones.

Dana eased off her brake. *If the car in front would just go,* she thought.

He raised his cardboard sign to his chest and came toward Dana. Rain fell. Dots speckled the sign. They tapped on her windshield. The driver in front of her finally released his brakes and moved. Dana stayed right on his tail, relieved.

She suppressed the urge to smile. As she passed the man, she looked up into his face just as he turned to go back to the beginning of his catwalk. Her breath caught. She turned to get a better look at that face. The car behind her came up tight so as not to miss the light and she had to make the turn. She looked back again, turning her shoulders. Her car climbed the tip of the median, then bounced down. Dana felt her hands trembling and tightened her grip on the wheel. She could only see the beggar's back now. The rain finally decided to drop in force and the man on the median seemed to dissolve into it.

"My God. My God," she said. She fought to control the wheel, then clamped a hand over her mouth. She couldn't act, couldn't think, having just looked into the face of her long-lost husband, thought dead these past nine years.

II. HAVE YOU SEEN ME?

Her car rocked to a stop in the parking space in front of her town house. She left the motor running; her foot smashed the brake.

That was him.

She knew that face. It could be disguised by scraggly hair and road dust and the exhaust of thousands of cars...yet the face she knew was there, lined by whatever had happened to him between the accident and now. She knew that face. She had pressed her face to that face. She had made that face laugh and made it cry. She turned the key to start the car and heard a cutting grind from the already running engine. Reynolds. Did he know she had moved? Did he know they were here? Checking behind her, she stepped on the gas and the car jumped forward. "Shit." She put it in reverse, but then slammed her brakes, causing the car to rock again on its chassis. This time she killed the engine, pulled her keys, and ran to her house. Inside, she called, "Frankie." He did not like "Frankie" anymore. "They call me Frankfurter in school," he had told her. "Franklin!" She called his name a few more times before running out the front door and shutting it behind her. She ran two doors down to her friend Brenda's.

The door opened to Brenda's smiling face. "Come get some spaghetti. It's just jar sauce, but we have some garlic bread."

"I'm sorry, Brenda. Accident on 28."

"Eh." Brenda waved the apology away as she turned, leading Dana to the kitchen.

"Hey, Mom."

Franklin and Brenda's two, Anthony and Nicole, sat at the kitchen table with tangled piles of spaghetti in front of them.

Dana kissed her son on the top of his head. When she straightened, she noticed Brenda looking at her.

Brenda mouthed, "What's wrong?" and beckoned Dana to follow her down the hallway.

In Brenda's empty family room, she said, "You look frazzled, like someone just ran over your dog. What's wrong?"

"The batteries died on my phone. I couldn't get ahold of Frankie."

Brenda crossed her arms and looked at Dana from under her eyebrows. "Please."

"I have to run out."

"Dana."

"It was that accident. The one that made me late. Freaked me a little. Look, I got to go. Will you hold on to Frankie for a few more minutes?"

"They're not done eating...where have you got to go?"

Dana was already moving down the hall. "Just an errand," she said over her back.

She said something about needing groceries, patted all three kids hurriedly, then ran back out into the rain. It wasn't until she was about to put her key in the ignition that she began to question herself. *Maybe it really was the accident that freaked me out.*

That panhandler had been Reynolds. But then, he had seemed too tall to be her husband. Yet, he had been standing on a concrete median, while she had sat in a car.

She looked toward her friend's home. The lights were on.

Everyone knows someone who looks almost exactly like someone else. She and her girlfriends used to describe men that way. What celebrity does he most resemble? Maybe she had just spotted a look-alike, nothing more.

There was one way to find out. She took a deliberate breath and started the car. Storm clouds now fully blacked the sky. The intersection where Reynolds had been standing was still busy with cars, but the median was vacant. She pulled into the gas station that occupied one corner. Dana fished her umbrella from under her seat. She stepped from her car, crossed the street, and walked south toward downtown, trying to see through the rainfall down both her side of the street and the opposite side as well. She had meant to go just a block or two, but ended up covering five. Despite the umbrella, the rain found ways to get at her. She looked in the windows of the diner and the fast-food restaurants she passed. The traffic was heavy and the cars sent spray over the sidewalk. No one else walked down this stretch of four-lane road where the posted limit was 25, but everyone did 40.

Dana stopped her search in the middle of a block. She could see very little, and hear only the rush-hour traffic and the drumming on top of her umbrella. She convinced herself to head back to her car.

Dana saw a man running from a little diner holding a folded newspaper over his head. He came directly up to her. He was clean shaven, with black hair.

"Do you need a ride?" he asked. He pointed over his shoulder, Dana presumed at his car. "It's getting nasty out here."

"Oh. No, thanks," she said and wasn't sure why she added, "My friends are waiting for me just a couple of blocks up the street. Thanks." She had to raise her voice to be heard over the rain.

"The weatherman got it wrong again. Does this feel like a 30 percent chance to you?"

Dana shook her head, tried to smile.

"Wish I had a job where I could be wrong so often." He peeked upward from under his paper. "Whew. My car is close," he said; it was a question.

"Have a good evening. Get dry." Dana walked briskly away. She glanced back after a dozen steps. The man with the paper was watching her. She quickened her pace, looked back again. He was gone.

She again peeked in the windows of the fast-food restaurants and the spaces between buildings. She imagined homeless people, if Reynolds was indeed homeless, squatting in cardboard boxes in narrow in-between spaces, waiting out the rain.

She climbed into her car and closed her umbrella after her like a crab folding into its protective shell. She locked herself in. The rain and the steamed-up glass completely obscured her view. Her wet clothes smelled. The back of her skirt and her stockings below the knee were soaked. Water trickled down her legs. She rooted about for a towel or napkin, but found nothing.

Oh, my God, Reynolds. You're alive? This is a fantasy. She wiped at the condensation on her windshield glass with a hand. She used to have these all the time, especially months after the accident, pregnant, exhausted, and grieving. Reynolds would come through the door. *I had to think about things,* he would say, *I had to think about our marriage. But now I'm back.* And all would be forgiven.

She drove back home, looking along the way at the drenched sidewalks and empty parking lots, at the medians between the streams of cars. When she stopped at a light she felt disappointment at not finding that man with the sign, and a little relief she chose to ignore. She sniffed, wiped tears, and worked to tamp down a hum of giddiness. She wanted to work up doubt, which would be reasonable, but there wasn't much doubt, not at that moment. Warren Reynolds, her husband, out there somewhere, clutching a cardboard sign while nickels jingled in his tattered pocket. Everything beyond the traffic light looked dark and haunted, as if there were large gaps in her known world, blank black spaces for which she could not account just beyond the headlights of the mindless cars.

Her survey of the buildings and the spaces between the buildings and the stretches of black asphalt fronting them continued during her ride home. She drove slowly the entire route. She imagined seeing the silhouette of the shaggy man with the large sign trekking on the shoulder of the road, heading toward her house. Not until then did she wonder if he knew where she lived; was that why he was so nearby, within walking distance of her neighborhood? Would he come see her? Was he coming to see Franklin? What did he know? Now fear grew, so much more immediate and intense than the giddiness or the relief. She turned the corner into the residential section. He was out there somewhere, not far at all.

She pulled into her parking space. Lights were on in her town house. The living-room light, the kitchen light, and, upstairs, the light from Franklin's bedroom all shone. She continually harped on him about leaving lights on in empty rooms. She even shook the electric bills at him one time, but she thought maybe she would let that particular battle go now. He was a latchkey kid; it was his way of filling up the rooms. He would turn on the TV in the living room too, even if he fixed himself a snack and went upstairs to his room to read. From outside, the house looked well occupied.

She left her umbrella in the car, choosing to dash to her front door. From the corner of her eye, she saw light from Brenda's door slice down her neighbor's front walk, but she inserted her key and pushed herself in before she could be hailed.

She exhaled loudly, feeling as if she'd just broken the surface after being held underwater. She slid the chain latch into place. Sometimes Franklin would use it and that would infuriate her as she would ring the doorbell and wait on him to come open the door. But the light and the shut door and the latch gliding into place felt welcoming, succoring.

"Franklin," she called, "did you get enough to eat?"

No answer. She sprinted up the stairs.

"Did you hear me?"

Franklin lay on his tummy with his chin propped in his hands, a fan of comic books and their chaotic colors in front of him. He wore his earphones. The MP3 player was at one elbow. He pulled an earphone out. "Hey, Mom," he said. "Iron Fist has been secretly posing as Daredevil."

"What?" Dana said, trying to emphasize the mocking tone. "I thought they were friends."

"They are. He's trying to help him protect his secret identity."

"Oh. Well...in that case."

Reynolds had read comic books from when he was a young boy well on into adulthood. He boasted of having a complete Iron Man set, including *Tales of Suspense*, whatever that meant. He had tried to get Dana interested, but she had balked, saying that every adult relationship should have at least one adult. As far as she knew, he'd kept reading his *Captain Americas* and *Spider-Men* until he died—no, disappeared. Franklin's enthusiasm was not an example of genetic stamping. Her son had found a cache of Reynolds's comic books at his grandmother's house and she had let him have some of them, and said the rest would be his when he was older. Dana had not understood why you had to be older to have comic books, and saw the woman's withholding of the books as a device to keep the boy wanting to come back.

Dana lingered in the doorway, watching her nine-year-old read. He had long lashes and an intelligent forehead. His nose was a perfect fit for his mouth and his eyes, his beautiful, bright eyes, which he leveled at her.

"What?" he said.

"Nothing, dear. Can't a mom look at her only son?"

"No. It's rude."

"I'm going. I'm going." She smiled but he was already back into the comic. She had picked one up once, just to check what her son absorbed so rapidly. It had seemed dark and unhappy, especially for something called a comic book.

She went to her room and kicked off her shoes. She sat on the edge of her bed massaging her feet. Her blouse was damp; she peeled it off, but then held it to her breasts.

In the next moment, she reached for the handset on her nightstand. She could report a missing person. Surely the police could find him. They knew where to look. Her mind pinballed. It had been the rain and the accident she saw on the way home; those were what had her thinking of Reynolds, seeing Reynolds. The specter was a trick of the rain and the red strobe lights. Maureen, his mother, had insisted he was alive. Dana tapped the handset softly against her lips.

———————

A milk carton sits on the kitchen table. The table is polished, and the reflection of the carton can be seen even in the dimmed light. There is a little boy's face on the carton. A local dairy put lost children's faces on the cartons then. Dana eyes the carton even while Steve is whispering in her ear.

He looks in her face for a reaction, but she has not heard him. A flicker of disappointment registers, but he smiles again and says, "You're lucky you don't have to go back."

"I said I had a doctor's appointment. You're just having a late lunch."

"A delicious lunch."

He takes her hand away from the lapels of her robe and parts it. She watches him look at her. Even though they have just made love, there is a thrill to this, him parting her robe and gazing at her. He gently caresses her right nipple. He is all touching, touching and tasting. He lowers his head to her breasts. His head is under her chin and she puts a hand lightly to the back of his head, tunneling her fingers through his long, gorgeous hair. His lips are skimming over her.

But something has intruded.

"You have a one o'clock," she reminds him, talking into his hair.

He puts an arm about her back to make sure she doesn't step away, but she wants him to leave, suddenly, she is sure he should go.

Forty-five minutes before, they had come bursting though the kitchen door, laughing and shoving. He had grabbed her from behind and she had crashed into the kitchen table. He bent her over it, pressing himself against her. The side of her face felt the cool, hard surface of the table until he jerked her up and around and began kissing her. They fumbled to the bedroom, but lost momentum once there. She had stepped back, just being playful, so that he would have to reach for her, but he had not come forward and there was a yard of distance between them. With the perspective of that gap, he became again a co-worker, who she sometimes saw in the teachers' lounge and sat across the table from in faculty meetings. *We can't set up the gymnasium for the play in advance; it's too cold to conduct PE outside.* And he had smiled at her while he said that, as if to say, see, even lowly PE teachers could detect the holes in that plan. They laughed together a lot. Of course, sometimes he tried too hard to be funny. They emailed and IMed a lot. "Did you see what vice-principal Murray was wearing? OMG!" She was conscious of the lines that were first straddled and then crossed. It all seemed like a sophisticated play. But he wasn't supposed to be touching her. And then once, when they were the last two exiting the lounge, he should not have put his hand to her belly. Another line crossed. And the first time they kissed. In her classroom, he pulled her by the wrist to the coat closet. He was being silly. They were laughing. And then they were not.

He kissed the palm she had held up. And then took the hand and pulled her to the bed.

Now, he wants to kiss her full on again, but she turns away. "C'mon," she says, intruding on the fantasy of his prowess and her seduction.

He tries to smile at the rebuff. Lunch period, after all, is over. The bell will be ringing. He says something about lunch and then tells her, "See you tomorrow," as if they just happen to be exiting their classrooms at the same time, like they're in the parking lot going to their cars. When he leaves, when she shuts the kitchen door and leans on it with both palms flat against its glass, she promises again that there will be no recurrence.

She is crashing now. She is perplexed with her behavior because she loves her husband. They have not been married long and sure, she is annoyed by his slow manner in performing any task and deciding any issue, and disappointed that he is perfectly content with movies as his primary entertainment, shrugging his indifference at the suggestion of parties or plays or concerts, but she is also fairly certain that what she has just done has little or nothing to do with any list of his strengths or shortfalls. She was prepared for a little guilt, that would be part of it, but this crash is coming quicker than she anticipated.

She had viewed the indiscretion as part of being young, as a little, private adventure just for her. No one would know, and years from now, she could imagine herself looking back on it and shaking her head at her wild, impetuous side. She'd be the matriarch of the clan and all her husbands would be buried and fondly remembered as she tells the story of her affair as a cautionary tale. "Grandmother, you didn't!" "Dumbest thing I ever did," she would admit, even though there were no real consequences, just a hammering guilt that evolved over the years into a hard-won wisdom.

Dana turns from the kitchen door. She hears Steve's car starting from the street. She can smell Steve on her, a combination of both of them, musky. She puts the heels of her palms in her eyes and breathes out. "No one needs to know," she whispers and a bit of the recent thrill returns, enough to make her feel a warm flush in her chest.

But then there is the little issue of the milk carton remaining. A gap-toothed boy with uneven bangs is asking, *Have you seen me?* She is certain she hasn't. She never pays any attention to the carton pictures, which look like any number of the hundreds of children at Oak Lane Elementary. She walks to the table and reaches for the milk, but her fingers curl away before contact. A sinking hollows out her chest. It's not the boy with the bangs at all. It's the carton. Because she is now sure, as sure as she is standing there looking for her next breath, that when Steve and she came bursting into the kitchen and made their way back to the bedroom, the carton had not been out on the table.

III. NECESSARY GIFTS

For some reason, Franklin climbed out of the pool, scurried over five feet of poolside, and jumped back in. Dana was held in suspense for those few moments he was under, though she had seen him disappear beneath the water hundreds of times, with nothing to mark his having been there except a rapidly dissipating froth of bubbles. It felt foolish to wait, to hold all other thoughts in abeyance until that black head erupted from the surface, which it did. He shot straight up, clearing the water almost to his waist. He must have shoved off from the bottom as he'd seen the other boys in the class doing. He looked around for his audience, but the instructor had called the boys over to the edge to practice their kicks while Franklin was under, and no one had stuck around to witness his feat. Upset, his eyes sought hers, but he contained himself. Perhaps he hoped she had not seen. She should have looked down at her magazine, she thought.

He swam to the side, where bubbly waves were being manufactured by half a dozen seven- to nine-year-old boys. Franklin held on to the edge but did not join the line until the instructor noticed and barked his name.

He often seemed to just miss in that way. His attempt to mimic the antics of the other boys, joining in too late. Though they had been called to the side, he would see their departure as a rebuff, and would be quiet and reserved for the rest of the swim lesson.

She had read the same line in her magazine article at least six times. She finally gave it up. The back of the magazine had a perfume ad with a model in a wedding dress. She rolled the magazine into a tube and stuck it in her bag.

When Reynolds had proposed, Dana took the ring and asked him if she could have a few days to think it over. Seeing the look on his face, already defeated, crestfallen, like a caged puppy watching you walk away, she kissed him on the cheek and said she wanted to think it over, but liked his chances. After the accident, she kept wearing the ring for nearly two years. It was still in her jewelry box, where it was supposed to remain forever. She was sure it still fit. Her thumb rubbed over her ring finger, feeling the absence of the band for the first time in a long time.

The children ran to the locker room. They were told no running and converted to a rapid walk that was nearly as reckless on the wet surface. Franklin was in the herd of shiny skinned boys who disappeared around the painted, concrete-block wall.

The pool was abruptly empty, but the water still rocked. The light bounced from the randomly generated facets of the pool's surface. Parents climbed down from the bleachers.

Franklin was one of the last to reappear. She wanted to say something to him about it, but said instead, "You did great." An old standard. If he ever called her on it, asked, what was so great about it, she wouldn't know what to say.

Mother and son walked to the car in silence.

"Do you want to go to McDonald's?" she asked.

"I'm tired of McDonald's."

"Since when?"

He didn't reply. His hair was still wet. Drips worked down his forehead and he looked as if he'd been perspiring heavily.

"You can make some hotdogs when we get home."

"We don't have any buns."

"You can use regular bread."

Her mother had died when Dana was three years old. Everyone tells her that this was simply too young to remember anything about her, but Dana swears to this day that she remembers two things. Outside on the patio, Dana is in the plastic wading tub and Mommy is sitting in a lounge chair in a bathing suit. (Her big sister contends that Mom never wore a bathing suit in the back-yard. Leslie dangles her superior memories of their mother over Dana's head, like an especially exquisite toy she has no intention of sharing.) In the wading tub memory, her mother is wearing sunglasses and turns to look at her, and Dana sees herself reflected in the oversized lenses. Her mother plucks her from the water and places Dana on Mommy's chest and then wraps her in a towel or blanket.

The other picture is also suffused with brightness. Again it is just the two of them. Mommy is standing at the window over the sink. The light from the window is horribly bright. Mommy hums a song and the soft humming has attracted Dana to her side. Dana remembers trying to hum along with Mommy and Mommy not noticing at first and then she turns and looks down directly at Dana. The light is filtering though her hair. She smiles. "That's right," she says and they hum together. The frustrating thing about this memory is that she can't make out her mother's face. The light is behind Mommy and her hair acts like a hood. She recalls the smile, though. She had told these memories to a boyfriend in college, who reminded her that the human brain at three is not developed enough to retain memories such as those, and that they were probably memories of another relative, or adaptations of anecdotes she had heard while young. She had dropped that boy a week later and became quite discriminating when it came to telling anyone what she remembered of her mother.

Once, during bedroom talk, she had told Reynolds of her memories of her mom. "What a gift," he had said in a whispered rush of enthusiasm. "It's everything you need from your mom, Dana. In one memory she is drying you off so you don't get a chill, protecting you, and in the other, she is encouraging you, you know, letting you know you can sing too."

Dana had nodded at this and wiped her eyes. "Leslie says, everybody says, I was too young to remember—"

"No," he said. "These were necessary gifts. You remember them, and just right."

In the car after swim class, Franklin asked, "Mom, I said, where are we going? This isn't the way home."

Dana had returned to Route 28 where it intersected with Liberia Avenue. Her head was turning from one side of the road to the other. The median and the sidewalks were empty.

"What are you looking for?"

"Hmm, honey? I thought we'd stop by the grocer. Get some buns."

IV. MAN UNACCOUNTED FOR

Finally, she spotted someone. After days of turning each commute into a manhunt, spending each spare moment driving around, searching, she saw someone in a dirty tan coat cutting between the vehicles in a used car lot. The traffic light just ahead turned red right at that moment and she had to slam on her brakes to avoid colliding with the car ahead of her. Her car's front end dived. There couldn't have been more than five inches between the bumpers. Dana cursed quietly. The driver of the other car seemed not to have noticed. In those scant seconds, the man she'd seen walking through the used car lot was gone. The light turned green and she pulled into a gas station and parked off to the side, away from the pumps and customer traffic.

She had left her son alone in his room with his comics practically all day. It was time to head home to him, but she had been telling herself that for the last hour. She had spotted few pedestrians today and none who gave a definite impression of being homeless—no signs, no panhandling. She climbed from her car and marched to the spot where she had last seen the man in the dirty coat. The sidewalks were dry, the concrete highly reflective and hard on the eyes. The road ran straight for nearly two miles. The man had to have slipped between the cars on the lot, lost behind all the glare of windshield glass. She stepped onto the lot and a salesman bolted from the trailer office. She raised a hand to stop him and quickly backtracked to the gas station. She pivoted in a spot several feet from her car. There was movement all about her, cars and people aimed in distinct directions.

She tried to avoid questioning herself. As long as no one knew what she had seen or what she thought she had seen, she could afford to indulge herself.

Reynolds alive. Warren Reynolds walking, breathing this entire time. While his wife and son, mother and sister, and friends had all suffered his loss. It had nearly killed his mother. Had he picked up the newspaper and read about the accident of October 8, 2002? She herself had seen it in the hospital while in a wheelchair parked in a hallway.

Man Unaccounted for in Bizarre Single-Car Accident

The count still stands at one injured and one missing in last night's car accident on Route 234 southbound at the Occoquan Bridge. Warren Reynolds, aged 24, and his wife, Dana, 23, of 1154 Jenkins Lane, Fredericksburg, Virginia, were proceeding home when Warren apparently lost control of his 1992 Toyota Camry on rain-slicked roads. The car tumbled down the embankment and was partially submerged in the Occoquan River.

Dana Reynolds was taken to Prince William Hospital, where her condition was graded at serious.

Mr. Reynolds has yet to be located. Neal Buhr, Captain, Prince William Volunteer Fire Department, stated that the current is fast and treacherous around the bridge and if Mr. Reynolds was ejected from the car, he could have been carried downstream.

Fire and rescue workers from Manassas are continuing a search begun at first light today.

Authorities have no evidence to suspect alcohol or drugs contributed to the incident.

She remembered the first paragraph exactly and some of the rest. Had he read that she was taken to the hospital and yet stayed away? No matter what she had done...had he been so angry that he would leave her trapped in a sinking car?

"Excuse me, ma'am, are you having car trouble?" A man was walking up to her, wiping his hands on an oily rag.

"No—"

"Well, you can't park there."

Dana considered asking if he saw many homeless around, and where they went.

He looked at her with impatience.

"I was going to grab a Coke inside," she said. "And some chips."

"That's okay," he said, but didn't allow a smile. "We saw you heading down the street..."

Dana walked by him to buy the soda she had committed herself to.

She had a picture of Reynolds in her purse. When she dug out her change for the soda she saw it. She had taken it from the family album late last night. The cashier, a short Sikh man wearing a white turban, held out his hand. Dana took out the picture, but then slipped it back into her purse. She found her change and dropped it in his hand. She took her soda and sat on a gray painted curb that skirted two sides of the building. It was intended, she supposed, just to protect the building from cars. It wasn't a comfortable perch, too narrow to make a good seat. The mechanic who'd questioned her was nowhere to be seen. She let her legs splay widely in front of her. It was a busy intersection for cars, but not for foot traffic. The endless streams of vehicles, even as they were apportioned by the traffic lights, flowed in ways that began to look less directed and more mindless. She had never just sat and observed traffic before without being part of it.

She checked her watch, noted the time, and promptly forgot it. She took the picture from her bag again. She had selected it because it was a good, clear head shot. Reynolds was smiling and looking at the camera. Little could be seen behind him, the outlines of a brick building with white shutters. She didn't think she had taken the picture. She had expected it to ignite some memory of a specific event, but it had not. She looked at the eyes of the man in the photo. *If you are alive, what the hell are you doing? What happened to you? Are you just drifting?* She tried to picture him standing on the median of the street in front of her. Cars flashed by from both directions. She saw him more as he was in the photograph and not as she had seen the man in the street. There was no room out there with people speeding by so quickly that a system of timed lights had to be constructed to get them to pause even for a minute. How well can you know someone? No better than you can know yourself. He had pretty brown skin.

Someone hurried across the street. It was a woman walking against the light, looking down the entire time. A car narrowly avoided her, the sound of its horn trailing after. Once she made the sidewalk she slowed down, even showing a limp. She came toward the gas station—in fact, she came straight toward Dana. From several feet away, Dana could hear the woman sniffling, and then the sound of a low whine. She wore a denim jacket and jeans, and an off-white sweatshirt under the jacket. Her hair was long and curly and very black. At first Dana couldn't tell if she was black or white or Hispanic, but then decided she was white. She had a seared, creased face.

"Oh! Damn it," the woman said and let herself drop on the same narrow skirt of concrete where Dana sat just four feet away. She snorted and droplets flew from her nose. Her eyes were veined red.

She turned toward Dana and fished into the front pocket of her tight jeans. Coins trickled out after her hand, which was balled around more coins and bills. The woman looked at the money sprouting between her fingers and then threw it down on the pavement.

Dana held her hands up defensively against the bouncing coins that speckled the space between the two women. She scowled at the woman and scooted another few inches away from her. The woman was rubbing her eyes and didn't notice either the look or the move.

The bills began to move along the asphalt, hesitantly, like little mice unsure they'd been given their freedom.

Dana watched as tears dangled from the woman's chin. Her long hair looked damp and oily and clung to the sides of her face.

When the dollars began to move faster, Dana snatched them. There were six singles, some balled tighter than Brussels sprouts.

The woman covered her face with her hands and cried into them.

Dana looked around, but no one else seemed to notice this scene, in which Dana had inadvertently involved herself by picking up the money. She unballed the money and attempted to flatten the bills by stretching them over her leg. When they were as flat as they were going to get, she folded them in half. She then began picking up the coins. She was working her way closer and closer to the distraught woman, who acted as if she didn't notice that someone was picking up her money.

"Hey, Miss," Dana said, holding out the money. "Your money. Your money."

The woman looked through her hair at Dana, with an expression that said she didn't understand what Dana was proposing. Finally she looked down at the hand holding out the mound of change and the folded bills.

"Thank you, honey. You givin' me these?" She had a husky, surprisingly heavy voice.

"It's—"

"I'll take it if you givin'...then it's just a gift."

The woman's dry fingers clawed the money from Dana, who wiped her hand on her jeans reflexively, belatedly thinking it may have been insulting to do so.

"You looked lost," the woman said. "Before, when you were standing over there." The woman pointed to a spot near Dana's car. She had not put her money away yet. "You new around here? Need directions?"

"No, I'm...I don't—" Dana stood, then stooped to retrieve her half-empty Coke bottle.

Squinting, the woman looked up. Dana couldn't place the woman's age. She could be 30 or 55.

Dana sat back down. It wouldn't do to have brought the photograph and not show anyone. She fished it out and held it toward the woman. "Are you around here a lot? Have you seen this man?"

The woman looked without focusing.

"His hair would be grown out and he has a beard, a thick, scraggly beard."

The woman stuffed her money into her pocket and leaned over the photo. Her hair smelled. She smelled. "Are you the cops?" She wiped her face in the crux of her elbow. "I'm askin'."

"No."

"Black feller." She grasped the bottom of the photo. Dana did not relinquish her hold on the top. "What do you want him for?"

"Does it matter?"

"Hell, yeah."

"He's...family."

"Family, well that can be the worse kinda trouble. See what I'm sayin'? Shit, family. And I wouldn't want to bring him grief; he's a nice guy." She wouldn't let go of the photograph.

"You know him then?" It occurred to Dana that the photo was ten years old now. Could someone really be identified from a decade-old photo? Faces are in a constant state of transformation.

"Yeah, sure. I know him."

Dana felt the jump again, the same one she'd experienced when she first spotted Reynolds under the traffic light.

"You have to be sure..."

"Like you said, he has hair all over now. Like a wild man, right?"

Dana pulled the picture from the woman's grasp and looked at it. "What's his name? What do you call him?" she asked.

"Same thing you do, I guess."

"You don't know him."

"Sure I do. Talk to him now and again. Name's Wendell."

The jump. Her throat constricted. It took a moment to ask, "Reynolds? Do you mean Reynolds?"

"Yeah, look, names are funny. Some people don't like to use them. Me? People can call me anything they want, and they have. Name's Jessie."

"Hi, Jessie. I'm Dana. Where is Reynolds? Do you know where he is?"

Jessie stretched her legs out and then stretched her hands toward her feet. Only then did Dana notice the raggedness of the woman's shoes. Their heels were flattened and a worn hole revealed her little toe.

The woman pretended, Dana thought, to be studying her hands, but Dana caught her flicking quick looks in her direction. She wondered if Jessie was homeless; she assumed she must be.

"Do you know where I could find him, Jessie?"

Jessie's eyes were watering. Her mouth quivered.

Dana wasn't sure what to say. She waited.

The mechanic returned.

"Ma'am, I'm going to have to ask you to move your car. Space is tight."

Dana looked at him and then with a tilt of her head indicated Jessie.

The mechanic did not look at the distraught woman. "Cars that are in for service—"

"I understand you."

"Then…" He made a gesture as if to say, then why is your car still there.

Dana stooped near Jessie, who was crying again.

"Do you need more money?" Dana asked. Without waiting for an answer, she dug into her purse and pulled out a ten.

The mechanic's hand shot up, its whorls and lines delineated with traces of oil. "No soliciting here."

Jessie sprang to her feet and, within inches of the man, her face reddened and stretched open. "I ain't soliciting for nothing, nothing!"

The mechanic looked at Dana as if to say, see what you've done now? He never acknowledged Jessie. "Panhandling, whatever. I don't need this. Try to be nice and this is what you get. I'm calling the cops and a tow."

Dana told the man's back she was leaving.

Jessie continued to shout. "Ain't soliciting."

Dana went to her car, putting a stiff-legged anger in every quick step.

She opened the passenger door for Jessie, who hopped in enthusiastically. "Whew," she said. "What an asshole, huh?"

Dana ran around to the other side without replying.

Jessie was sitting with one leg under her.

The odor in the contained space was nearly overwhelming. Dana caught her breath. It was a sour, funky, moldy stink.

"Show me where Reynolds is."

"Dear, there's a couple of places. I'm hungry as can be. Thirsty too. Can we go by Denny's?" She looked around the car as if she had not been in one before. She seemed to have forgotten whatever had caused her tears.

Dana rolled down her window and held a hand to her nose.

———

The faces of the other diners kept turning in their direction, their noses scrunched up. Dana got the feeling Jessie sensed them, but she did not acknowledge the scowls in any meaningful way. A practiced obliviousness, Dana thought. Jessie ate her eggs with gusto and ordered more. She sipped her coffee and glanced at Dana with a homely smile.

The waitress frowned at first and then became surly. She shot Dana looks, as if she should do something about it. Later, Dana saw her talking to the manager. He looked their way, but seemed disinclined to do anything.

The woman in the booth directly behind Jessie scooted from her bench in a huff. The man with her didn't seem aware of what was going on, but she coaxed him to his feet with a combination of looks and gestures. They took their plates and glasses and moved to another table.

Jessie was chattering about a church to which she once belonged and something about choir robes. Dana wasn't really listening, distracted by the hostility in the room. She only knew the woman wasn't telling her where Reynolds might be found.

"Perhaps we should go, Jessie," she said.

"I need to use the restroom," Jessie said. "I'm going to wash my face."

Dana waited.

What would she say to him, if she found him? If he were standing in front of her, maybe with that sign, and she walked up to him? What would be the first thing? She couldn't imagine him as the bristle-faced panhandler she'd recently seen, but as her Reynolds, a sensitive man with sensitive, sad-boy eyes and a clean-shaven face, full lips, and that strong jawline she always liked that looked more confident than his eyes. She took his photo out of her purse. There he was, looking back at her again. When was this picture taken?

"Ma'am?" the waitress said. She had a plastic pitcher of iced tea in one hand and a subtle, triumphant smile. "If you're waiting for your friend, she left a couple of minutes ago."

▼. GHOSTS OF LIVING MEN

One morning, months after her husband had disappeared, Dana Reynolds walked into her closet and stopped short. "Reynolds?" she asked, aloud. For a long time she stood as still as a deer, sensing that someone else was there nearby. Listening. She heard the whispery static hiss from the monitor that eavesdropped on Frankie, bundled in his crib. Beyond that, she heard neighborhood traffic from the street outside, a distant sound of people unfairly going about their normal lives making grocery store runs or picking up children from soccer practice. She stood there. Finally, she realized what held her. It was his presence, just behind her, lurking at her ear. She turned and saw his outline repeated in a row—his clothes, the scent of which had first arrested her. His shirts and pants and jackets, his things, his deodorant and aftershave, his sweat. Maybe she would even find hairs on the shoulders and collars of his coats and jackets, thin coils, and the scents where once there was a whole man. There was the tan camel-hair sport coat she had bought him. She had told him he could wear it to business interviews and meetings with his boss. She had liked the cut about his shoulders and the way it looked on him, or the way it made him look. He had not taken her advice. He wore the coat not only for special days, but all the time, even when it began to look thin at the elbows.

She stepped into the curtain of his clothes between the sport coat and his dress shirts. She drew them to her, hearing only the scooting hangers and then a soft silence. She closed her eyes. She felt him encircling. Her breath caught in her throat. He would greet her with an embrace each evening when they were both home again after a long day. His arms, the pressure on her back, his scent, the breath above her ear. Those hugs had become ritual for her. A few times she had rolled her eyes. But other times she had closed her eyes tightly. And toward the end, she had waited anxiously to find out if there would still be a hug.

The child monitor began reporting intermittent whines, which would build to urgent cries if she did not get to the nursery in time. She inhaled Reynolds's scent and opened her eyes.

She emerged from the curtain of clothes satisfied in the knowledge that her husband was dead.

Franklin whined about not having seen his grandmother since the summer. "She's old," he would remind Dana.

Reynolds's mother had called to tell him that a pineapple upside-down cake had been baked, a whole one just for him, and that it was waiting on her kitchen table.

That meant a trip south to Fredericksburg and an entire Saturday afternoon spent in the company of her mother-in-law, Maureen, and, of course, her sister-in-law, Ness Reynolds Macklin.

Reynolds had not grown up in Fredericksburg, but spent his high school years there, so he claimed it as his hometown. He told stories about playing in the Rappahannock. They had swam in it and built flimsy rafts, and later they would drink beer down by the water and fling the bottles into the night waters, listening for the splash. It seemed each summer they'd hear of a little boy who'd drowned in that river. The irony did not escape her; she did not look at rivers without thinking about currents and undercurrents and things forced under, enfolded, covered, and swept away. They played Civil War battles down there at the branch-strewn waterline where their teachers had told them the Union forces let themselves get bunched up with no sure route of retreat. Throughout the town, the teachers had said, those who stayed could hear the screams of men and gunfire down every street and alleyway. He and his friends hunted for souvenirs as every generation before them had and once in a while came across a corroded Minie ball or disfigured uniform button. Dana remembered Reynolds pointing out the steel cheek of a cannonball embedded in the worn brick of an old shop building. It was a killing ground down by the river, he had told her, the water stained red. And again she saw boys, face down, floating away on the indifferent water.

They crossed the Rappahannock on Route 1. Franklin asked if his Aunt Ness would be there. She said she didn't know. Ness Reynolds Macklin was her husband's big sister. She was the protective pit bull of the clan. Dana hoped they would miss Ness.

They drove into Fredericksburg, a city of less than 20,000 that was far enough away from Washington not to be a bedroom community. When they were well within city limits, Dana began thinking about what she should say. She had no real thought of sharing her secret with Maureen. Assuming Maureen did not already know. She did play a little with the idea of telling them. She could put it in their ear casually, like an oh-by-the-way thing. *Saw someone who looked like Reynolds the other day,* she might say, as anyone might mention seeing an old acquaintance. *Dead ringer, looked him right in the eyes. He looked like hell, by the way.* But that would have been an outright lie; she did not believe she had seen someone who *looked* like Reynolds.

Dread mounted in Dana as she recognized familiar streets and corners. Her son stared out the window. They should have come down more often for visits. It should have been no big thing for Franklin to see his grandmother. It should be easy. *Here we go,* she said to herself. *Here we go again.*

————

Dana's heart stops in the hospital. She is in pain and overwhelmed and wants nothing but sleep after having delivered Franklin. She named the baby Franklin for her father, as she had promised herself she would do. Franklin was born entirely white. His complexion had shocked Dana, who had imagined she would give birth to a heavily creamed coffee child. She is aware her mind is working in a bog of exhaustion and drugs. She tries to remember. They had been careful, she and Steve. Maybe there had been a time, a less cautious second go-round; she tries to recall, but finds she does not have the energy. Then Maureen and Ness explode into the room. Dana braces herself.

Maureen is crying. Tracks line her cheeks. Mother and daughter talk over each other. They always do. Dana does not have the strength to sort it out. But they have seen the baby. *Baby Warren,* Ness calls him.

"He looked at us and yawned," Ness says. "Do you want us to have somebody fetch him?"

Maureen says, "I see my boy in him. He has Warren's mouth and around the eyes...the eyebrows." Her face twists. She swallows and forces a wavering smile that looks sadder than the tears. "How are you, honey?" she asks.

Baby Warren. Little Warren. It was a week before she got up the nerve to tell them his name was Franklin.

"Look at the house," Franklin said.

Dana was looking about for Ness's car. And then another thought caught hold of her: What if he is here? What if this invitation to Franklin is actually a staged reunion? What if he and his scraggly beard and his cardboard sign are at the kitchen table right this second and Maureen is at the window saying, *Baby, they're here, they just pulled up*? Had he recognized her the same moment she had spotted him? Did he know she knew he was back? She parked in front of the Reynolds house.

Maureen would have told him about Franklin. He would return for the boy's sake if not for Dana's. Ness would be there too. The three of them would be waiting with string tied to a stick, the box propped up just so.

Dana did not see Ness's car and felt more encouraged as she climbed out.

Maybe I don't believe it was him I saw, Dana thought. *If I did, I would have told the police or I would at least want to tell his mother and sister. They could help me find him.*

They headed up the sidewalk. Her hand sought Franklin's, but the boy skipped ahead of her. "Slowpoke," he said and then repeated, "Look at the house."

The front gutter was falling away from the porch roof, a white slash, and the part of the gutter that wasn't down had green plant life growing from it. In places, the house paint was curled and cracked. Weeds in the front yard, some brown and dead, were knee high. Dana tried to recall their last visit here and if she had noticed any of the deterioration before.

"Franklin..." she said, but didn't quite know what to say next. He was up the porch steps. She no longer envisioned Reynolds inside waiting for them.

Franklin was knocking. "We have to fix that," he said. "We have to fix that, okay?" He knocked again. "Grandma, it's me and Mom."

They heard an answering voice. It sounded a long way off. They heard nothing else until the metal snaps of the locks.

Maureen looked as exhausted as her house. But she wore a huge smile on her face at the sight of her grandson.

Franklin immediately asked her about the gutter.

"That happened last night," she said.

"I can go on and pull it down," he said.

"Hello, Dana, how are you?"

"Good. Strong winds last night?"

"Some would say. I heard the entire house rattling. It sounded for all the world like devils trying to find their way in, trying any crack or crevice they could. Beating at windows and stomping on the roof. But this is a surprise. Come on in. Come on in. Come on in, Franklin, you can tackle that later."

Maureen's and Dana's eyes met. Dana could have sworn there was a message there, or maybe she was just projecting.

"I'm glad you could finally break loose and come down and visit an old lady."

"Don't start," Dana said. And she thought, *No, Maureen doesn't know anything about Reynolds returning.*

They went past the plastic-coated living room, reserved for vacuum-cleaner salesmen and insurance agents, to the kitchen, where there was indeed a cake topped with six yellow circles of pineapple sitting on the table.

"Can we have some now?" Franklin asked.

His grandmother said of course, whatever he wanted, and she moved slowly to a kitchen drawer and produced a knife. "You're old enough that it won't spoil your supper," she said in order to head off any protest from Dana, and handed the knife to him.

Maureen was wearing a wig of dark brown hair. Her natural color was black. It looked like a helmet spun of brown fishing line. Dana cut her eyes from it when Maureen looked her way.

"Tell me about school," Maureen said.

Dana thought her mother-in-law was asking her at first.

But to her surprise, Franklin unwound a long speech about his classes and friends and things he enjoyed doing and what he found boring. He described people and what they were like, how he had a teacher whose eyes never stopped blinking, that he'd earned the highest grade in the class on an essay test, and that French Club "only had two boys and like a dozen girls" in it so he was thinking about dropping it. It was his life, and it was more than he'd ever said about it to Dana.

She stayed at the table longer than she wanted, listening to her son's stories.

Dana bit into the square of cake Franklin had handed her and found it moist but too sweet. Franklin loved it and had his with milk. Dana slipped from the table and went back to the front of the house to look over the brown lawn. She used to fear this house after Reynolds had disappeared. It was full of a past no one could do anything about—not even, it seemed, let it go. She thought of the ghost of Jacob Marley and the rattling links he'd forged in life. It was like that. Maureen, who was convinced her son was not dead, had wanted to do nothing but talk of him and make plans to look for him. "There's a reason they ain't found the body. You'd think you'd be happy," she used to say. That was the first year or two.

Dana had wanted to explain about the day she had stood in her closet and felt certain that the ghost of Warren Reynolds had embraced her one last time, the palpable feel of the muscles of his arm, that she had not been asleep at the time so it could not have been a dream. Living men, she wanted to tell her mother-in-law, do not have ghosts.

There. There was spirituality for them. Dana had once told Maureen after a church service that she believed herself a spiritual person, but not a religious one.

Maureen had said, "That's what people say when they don't believe anything, but are too scared to admit it."

Dana had needed to have her husband declared dead in order to receive the $120,000 of life-insurance money. But Maureen had fought her on this at every turn. "Just an ounce of faith," Maureen

had said, "and you wouldn't need that money." Ness had sided with
Maureen, of course, even though Dana sensed she believed her
brother was gone as well.

"Mo, why isn't he back? Where is he?" Dana had long since
given up calling Maureen Reynolds "Mo," the name which at one
time had been, for her, an abbreviation for "Mom."

"Maybe he's sick, I think."

Dana could feel the accusation.

Ness would look at her too. "Is there a reason he wouldn't come
back?" she once asked.

Dana heard her son laughing from down the hall.

But maybe Maureen had been right. Dana thought, *Okay, self-
righteous Mama Reynolds was right, mean biddy...you were right.
But he hasn't come down here to help you paint this place or repair
gutters, has he?*

In a way, Dana felt, it had been about race. Because the white
woman wasn't spiritual enough to believe. The white woman was
too ready to hold services and to move on, and did not show the
faith they had; she could not believe in miracles as they did, was
unable to defeat the improbable with a simple dose of faith, evidence of things not seen. But as months turned into years, it wasn't
about Maureen's faith; it was about her ability to live in, to wallow
in, denial. So Dana had concluded.

They had taken her to their church when Reynolds and she were
engaged. It was an all-black church, and Dana was sure it was some
kind of test. Ness kept a portion of an eye on her the entire time.
Maureen, Ness and her latest boyfriend, Reynolds, and Dana had
all sat in a row. Reynolds had dutifully handed hymnals to all his
women. Dana had tried to look comfortable. She had sung along
with everyone, followed their cues. She had kept her face toward
the pastor, nodding her agreement at appropriate times, trying to
tunnel her attention, and had felt betrayed by the pastor when he
asked all visitors to stand so that they might be welcomed by the
congregation—the church family, he called it.

"Half stared at me like I was something from the zoo and the other half fought hard to not look like they were staring."

Reynolds had said, "Eye daggers. But they were aimed at me."

"I don't want to go back."

"Dana! It's like anything else. You get used to them. They get used to you. You may find friends there before long."

Dana thought, *If you were getting the disapproving looks and you've been going there for nearly eight years, then when will they accept me?*

They never returned.

She went back to the kitchen through the dining room and leaned on the refrigerator just inside. Maureen noticed her, but kept her attention on her grandson, who was telling another story. He was quite the chatterbox.

What had Reynolds become, Dana wondered. What do I really know that I could tell these two? If he was capable of letting his mother and sister suffer through the pain of his loss, he was no one she would want around her or her son.

After a while they went outside. Franklin immediately attacked the downed gutter, heaving.

"Careful, Franklin," Dana said and looked to Maureen to tell the boy to stop.

"The edges dig into my hands," Franklin said. He inspected his cupped hands. He had not been cut. "I need gloves."

Maureen told Franklin to wait a second. She went inside and came back after a moment with a towel. "Wrap this around it, so you won't cut yourself."

Dana made an impatient exhalation.

Maureen said, "What? He'll be okay. He's my big boy now."

Franklin avoided looking his mother's way and wound the towel around a part of the gutter. He renewed his tugging with loud grunts.

A gentleman from across the street came with a ladder. Maureen called him Mr. Vidi. "How are you holding up today, Miss Mo?" he asked. "I've been meaning to get over here and offer to see if we could get that back up." She introduced her daughter-in-law and her grandchild.

Mr. Vidi said to Franklin, "Let's see if we can't tack this thing back up there. And if we can't, then we'll haul her down, all right? All right."

He began to open his ladder.

Maureen said, "Dana, come back in and get the rest of the cake for Franklin. I'll wrap it in some plastic wrap or foil or something."

Dana hesitated, then followed Maureen back into the house. She tried to position herself where she could see her mother-in-law and keep an eye on her son. She didn't know the man out there and she did not want Franklin climbing the ladder. She stood in the hallway. She couldn't see Franklin, but she could hear them and she could see part of the ladder.

Maureen's wig looked shiny, not lustrous shiny but synthetic, cheap shiny. *Hope she doesn't think she's fooling anyone,* Dana thought. *Some black women can wear the most unrealistic hair pieces.* Franklin's hair coiled, but with a lot less tension. Dana had been afraid she wouldn't know how to maintain it. It was beautiful hair. Maureen had said it was good hair. Dana wasn't sure what that meant.

Maureen picked up a glass from the kitchen table. "More?" she asked.

Dana shook her head. She could hear the man's voice. "The wood is rotted right here. The nail didn't have anything to bite into." She didn't hear Franklin's reply.

Maureen returned the glass to the same spot on the table. She shook her head. "Thanks for bringing my grandson down. How he's changed. It don't take kids no time at all, does it? Always growing and changing."

"Yes, he's going to be tall too. If I can just get more meat on him…"

Maureen measured out a sheet of foil. "This is the best afternoon, best day, I've had in a long time." She looked up at Dana.

"Well…good."

"He's my family, Dana."

Dana felt a physical reaction. She felt her body tighten from legs to chest. She had almost begun to believe she might escape this. Emotional ambush.

"It ain't right you use him like this," Maureen said. "He's my family too. Him and Nessy are all I got." She stopped fussing with the foil and let herself drop into one of the kitchen chairs, looking exhausted.

"I'm not using my son." *Here it is,* Dana thought. "You've resented me—" Dana glanced down the hallway and then back to Maureen and lowered her voice. "You have something to accuse me of every time I come over here."

Maureen said, "This game don't play anymore, okay? I never tear off enough foil. You'd think I'd know by now."

"What game, Maureen?"

"Please."

"What game?"

"The one where you don't allow my grandson to visit just out of spite and venom."

"Spite and—listen, Mrs. Reynolds," Dana heard a voice tell her to shrug and walk away, to just go check on Franklin, even as her face heated. "I work for a living. I teach. I have a busy schedule and cannot always find the time to haul us down here. Franklin has school and after-school clubs and…you know what, Maureen? Last I checked, Route 1 has a northbound lane. Imagine that. Runs in both directions."

Dana crossed her arms.

Maureen looked unfazed by the sarcasm.

"I'm to blame for every bad thing in your life, aren't I? I take Reynolds and now I take Franklin."

"I want to know if Reynolds knew you were pregnant before the accident."

"What does that have to do—"

"Had you told him yet? You must have been two months or more along by then…"

"Why are you changing the subject?"

"Did he know?"

"No. I've already told you that, years ago."

"Why didn't you tell your own husband y'all were gonna have a child, hmm?"

"Next time you wonder why we don't come visit, Mo, you remember this."

Dana was almost to the front door. She could see that the gutter had been reattached. Mr. Vidi and Franklin were looking at something near where a porch column met the porch roof. Her hand was on the door. She turned around. She felt every step back down the hallway, but, as she would recall it later, it would seem as if she had spun around and was face to face in front of Maureen as she rose from the kitchen chair.

"I got something to tell you. You were right about one thing. I shouldn't have had Reynolds declared dead. I was trying to get the insurance money for Franklin's college and to pay the damn rent. But you fought me on it. You were right. You had me there, girl, because just last week I saw Warren. I saw your precious. There he was, big as day, not five feet from me!"

The woman's eyes. No, Maureen had not known Reynolds was alive.

"What? He hasn't been by here to see you? Hasn't been working on the gutters? Guess I'm keeping him away too. You want to see Franklin again, you know where we live."

She told Franklin it was time to go as she hurried down the porch steps. From inside the car she saw him shaking hands with the neighbor. Franklin looked from the car to Maureen's front door. Dana squeezed the steering wheel. Maureen did not come out. Minutes passed and finally her son appeared carrying his foil-wrapped cake.

He asked before getting in the car, "What did you do?"

"Get in."

"Mom, what did you say?"

Dana shook her head. "She's just mad because we don't come around enough to suit her, honey," Dana said.

———————

She sits in Maureen's living room in a stiff wingback that wears a noisy, protective vinyl casing. It sticks to Dana's forearms and the backs of her thighs. Upon stepping through the front door, Warren had placed Dana in Ness's care and raced upstairs to change his shirt. Their date, which was supposed to be lunch and hanging out downtown, has been extended to include a dinner celebrating a cousin opening her own clothing boutique. Ness leads her into the living room, chatting politely, then leaves her there. Evening is falling at the windows and the living room dims. The only strong light comes from the kitchen down the hall. Dana had been under the impression they would meet the other members of the dinner party at the restaurant, but she hears voices from the kitchen indicating they have already gathered. People are talking over each other and laughing. Abruptly there is quiet, tailed by a line of whispering. Then she hears giggling. The isolation is acute. In a few minutes, Maureen, Ness, and the others all come forward. Warren bounds down the stairs.

It's such a small thing, yet she remembers it always.

▼I. WATER, WATER

She woke soaked through her gown. Disoriented, she felt around the damp sheets. She wondered if she had wet the bed. Her hair was lacquered to her face and neck. She sat up, feeling a chill as her damp skin met the room's cool air.

She wished Franklin were near and thought of going to his room and sitting in his chair, watching him sleep. There had been a dream. In the dream, there had been water and it seemed the water had followed Dana back to the real world. She shivered. At

———

first, she did not remember the dream except for the water and the residual uneasiness.

She pulled the damp nightgown over her head. Ignoring the cold on her skin, she pulled the sheets from the bed. Reynolds. He had been in the dream. And water and darkness, she remembered that too. She flicked on the bathroom light, but shielded her eyes from it. Naked, she walked across the cold tile floor to the shower. She turned on the shower, hoping the rush of water through the pipes would not wake her son.

Some morbid streak kept forcing her to retrieve that dream, which she sensed was a nightmare and better left forgotten. When the shower stream was sufficiently hot, she stepped in. The heat and the steam were comforting and rinsed the clamminess from her body. She thought she heard a noise like the creak of a stair and leaned out of the spray, listening to nothing.

"Franklin?" she asked quietly.

She was embarrassed by the skittish crack in her voice. She returned to the water.

As soon as she immersed her head, turning her face up to the pins of water, the entire nightmare flooded her consciousness.

The front half of their car is submerged. The hood disappears into black, lapping water. Reynolds's face is at the passenger side window, his nose flat against the glass. His breath plumes steam against it. He's grinning like a clown, like a crazy man. He's looking around the cabin of the car but doesn't seem to see her. Steam and blood come from his flattened nose. His grin shows bloody teeth and gums. He presses a palm to the glass. Water runs from the white palm. His wild face stuns her, though she is also aware of wrestling with the seat belt. Unable to release it, she is also afraid to get out of the car. He spots her at last; he's angry and begins slapping the glass with his hand. The window begins to crack under his slaps; an intricate web of cracked glass fans out farther with each blow. The river is now up to the windshield and she can feel that her feet and ankles are underwater. She struggles with the belt. She shouts at him, feels her throat ripping raw with her shouting.

He stops hitting the glass. He grins. Water is leaking into the car, down the door, onto her lap from where he has cracked the glass. He backs away. She can hear the water around his legs. He backs into the river. His eyes aren't focused on anything. He turns and heads into the black, swirling river. She shouts. She doesn't remember what she is shouting. She doesn't want him to go into the water, but she doesn't want him to come back either, not the way he looks now. She knows if he could hear her he would turn back around. The water is pouring in now even though the window has not shattered. She loses sight of Reynolds. She cannot see through the cracked glass. Something floats by her ankles.

She woke up soaking wet.

Reynolds's wild face had her shaking.

She stood in the hot shower, just letting the stream rush over her. The water crowded her senses, isolated her from everything outside and, too, she dreaded the chill she would get when she turned it off. She was trying to forget the nightmare now that she had dredged it up. She used to have nightmares of the accident all the time—not the first year following, but the second and third years. Those were different than this one. Those had been brief and mostly had to do with the car flying off the road and bouncing down the embankment.

She did not think she could go back to sleep. Besides, she had pulled the damp sheets from her bed. It was still dark at the bathroom window. She wondered what time it was. It was that curiosity that coaxed her from the shower.

She heard the tail end of a noise as soon as the shower was off. Her hand held the knob and she listened for it again. A heavy grating sound, not the usual creaks of the house.

"Franklin, honey?"

Dana stepped from the shower and grabbed her towel. She tiptoed. *What was that,* she asked herself, but could not place the sound. She made no effort to dry herself. In her bedroom, she felt about on the floor with her foot and found the panties where she'd kicked them off. She did not turn on the light. She could not find her top, so she wrapped the towel tightly about her chest and tucked it securely.

At her bedroom doorway, she waited, listening, and heard nothing but the hum of the refrigerator from the kitchen. She crept to Franklin's room and eased his door open enough to peek in. She could make him out curled in the middle of his bed, breathing softly.

She felt better and maybe a bit braver for having seen him. She tried to go down the stairs quietly. But her own house was giving her away by creaking with every other step. She wished she had a gun. She didn't believe in them, but they were reassuring to scared people and she counted herself amongst their number.

Her hands went over the front door lock. She found a heavy vase in the living room and held it by its neck like a mallet until she crept into the kitchen and exchanged it for the butcher knife. She had already begun to relax. Her eyes were adjusted to the darkness now and she could see every colorless thing. The noise had not repeated itself. Still, she did not turn on the lights. She looked in the powder room and the pantry.

The towel fell away. "Damn it," she said quietly, picking it up and holding it against her chest.

Only the basement remained to be checked. She hesitated at the top of the stairs, looking at the dark hole before her. Her fingers touched the light switch. She wondered if it would be smarter to turn on the lights and thus announce her arrival, or to slip down using the same dark cover the possible intruders were using. She waited, imagining someone else down there amongst her boxes and Franklin's toys waiting for her to come down. She thought she was being silly now. If she went back to bed she could get another half-hour or forty-five minutes of sleep before it was time to get up for good. She flicked on the basement light.

There was the noise again.

Quicker, briefer this time. It did not come from the basement in front of her, but from behind her, the kitchen or the backyard. She ran to the kitchen door.

One of her patio chairs was vibrating.

Dana peeked from behind the door's translucent café curtains. Light from the narrow basement window spread across the ground a few yards from the house, mostly across the rough pebbled surface of the patio, then faded short. The light threw shadows from the kitchen steps and the patio furniture into the yard. She saw nothing at first and then caught her breath. A dot of light shone under the black umbrella of the tulip tree. Just as she spotted it, it dropped from about five feet above the ground and disappeared, a tiny meteor. A cigarette.

Dana turned from the door's glass. Someone was out there. Someone had been sitting on her patio smoking. Someone had scooted a chair across the rough surface.

She wanted to shout, *Get the fuck out of my yard.* She wanted to say that she had called the police. She wanted to move. Her lips would not move. Her screaming mind was disconnected from her paralyzed body, and wouldn't heed the panicked signals it was sent. Finally, a slurred squeak came from her that she hardly recognized. The person under the tree must have heard it. Dana saw movement. A figure moved from near the trunk, running away from the house. The figure vaulted the back fence. She brought her hands to her face, forgetting the knife was still in her hands, and nicked herself just above the right eyebrow.

She dropped the knife and then hopped from one foot to the other as it clattered near her.

She checked that the door was locked. Clutching her towel in front of her, she ran to the front door and checked it again. She ran back to the kitchen, to the window over the sink that looked out on her backyard. The chair was still. The branches of the tulip tree waved in the evening breeze.

Water from her hair trailed over her shoulder blades and down her back.

She retrieved the knife. She sank down to the floor with her back to the kitchen cabinet. Light from the lamppost made the knife blade gleam. The blade was trembling.

VII. ROCKING CARS

If Warren Reynolds knew where his family lived, that changed everything. Now Dana had to wonder if she had anything to fear from him. He had never been a violent man. But then, he hadn't smoked cigarettes either.

It had taken a while for her to get ahold of herself that night. She was surprised at how immobilizing the panicky feeling had been. It felt as if she had sat on the kitchen floor for hours before pulling herself up using the kitchen counter and picking up the phone. It was too late to dial 911. She dialed Brenda's number. Brenda's husband answered in a groggy, unintelligible murmur.

"Geoff it's me, Dana—"

He handed her off.

"Hello? Mama?"

"It's Dana. Someone is in my backyard...well, they were. Someone was in my backyard."

She heard an intake of breath.

"Lock all the doors, honey. Did you call the cops?"

She could hear Geoff's voice too. He wanted to know what was going on.

"I think he's gone, but I'm not sure."

Then she heard Brenda saying, more faintly, "Where do you think you're going?"

"Dana," Brenda said back into the receiver again. "Geoff is going out to our back deck to look into your yard.

"Tell him to be careful."

"Why didn't you call the cops?"

Dana was looking out the kitchen window at the heavy shadow under the tree. "Because he's already gone, I think. I'm not even sure he was trying to get in."

"So? He was in your backyard!"

"Brenda, I'm so scared. Thank goodness Franklin is asleep. I think he slept through it."

Geoff and Brenda came over minutes later, after Geoff had satisfied himself that no one was lurking about. Dana had pulled on a robe by then, but still had the kitchen knife. Dana took her friends through the whole thing from the scooting noise she heard while in the shower to the flare of the cigarette she saw under the tree. She was saved from telling them what she thought was the most important part—her suspicion regarding the lurker's identity—by Franklin coming down the stairs.

"What's everybody doing here?" he asked, rubbing his eyes.

Dana said, "Their electricity went out and they came over to see if ours was too."

Brenda arched an eyebrow at Dana.

Franklin went to the living room window. "But your lights are on," he said.

"Are they?"

"Hey! That's great. They're back on." Brenda clapped. "Well, I guess we can get going."

Franklin said, "You should get a camping lantern so you can still read when the lights go out."

———————

Dana was driving slower than the speed limit down Route 28.

Franklin was at Brenda's with a fresh stack of comic books.

On Route 28, behind the McDonald's and the mom-and-pop diner and the cleaner's and the Exxon, was a practically hidden trailer park. Driving past, Dana was scanning parking lots and the spaces between buildings. She was seeing stores and spaces she had never noticed before, even though she commuted down this very road. It was an ugly stretch of street, marked by abandoned houses that had been converted into payday-loan businesses, to pay for the used car from the ubiquitous lots, and the used tires from the used tire stores for your new used car. It was a four-lane road, but the speed limit was a revenue-generating 25 miles per hour. Peripherally, she saw that the car in front of her was not moving, the distance between them shrinking to nothing just as she slammed her brakes. The tap did not set off her airbag and for a moment she hoped she had avoided a confrontation. But a man climbed from the car and focused on her through her windshield. He gave her a gesture that she interpreted as, *Well, are you okay?* She nodded, twisted her lips in disgust, and stepped from her car.

She said, "I hadn't realized you'd stopped."

"That's generally what I do when the car in front of me stops. I recommend it." He was an older man with paint-splattered jeans and dusty boots.

"I'm so sorry," she said. "I am insured."

Cars were slowing around them. She was aware of being gawked at.

"Yeah, but I don't know where I'd put the money."

Only then did she examine his car, which was a flat, molting brown color that looked as if it had never seen a bottle of car wax. His bumper was damaged, but she thought it couldn't have all been her doing. Most of the dents already had scabs of rust delineating them.

"Five dollars and we'll call it even," he said.

She looked at his red face in surprise. "Oh, okay. Let me get my purse."

"Hah, I'm just kidding. Hah." He waved her away and dropped back into his car.

After that, she conducted her search on foot. She parked her car in the Food Lion's lot. Her front license plate was bent in the middle.

While walking, she got a better look at the trailer park that she had not known was there. There were places to hide from view everywhere. If whole neighborhoods can be hidden, one man could disappear at will. Gaps in fences, backyards, narrow alleys, abandoned buildings. Was he in the area because he knew Dana and Franklin had moved here? Was he already watching her, hanging out in her backyard?

The highway became Center Street, which was the main vein through old downtown Manassas. As in Fredericksburg, huge Civil

War battles had been fought nearby. Northerners called the biggest of those the Battle of Bull Run, which had poetic flair. Southerners called it First Manassas. It had been the first large fight of the Civil War. It was here where the entire country had realized the war was not going to be easy, and that they were in more trouble than they had allowed themselves to fear. Manassas, unlike surrounding towns that were actually suburbs dotted with strip malls, was a real town, with a downtown featuring banks, shops, a barber, churches, and an antique train station.

There had been another battle called Second Manassas, if Dana recalled correctly. In each case, the Southern forces had carried the day. It was Third Manassas that was beating them now, as the bedroom communities of Washington, DC, invaded the small town and slowly changed the climate, with housing prices going up. Large numbers of Hispanics had moved in too. Manassas had been a good secret: an affordable part of northern Virginia. That was changing.

Dana walked several blocks into the small downtown. She didn't know what she expected to find and fought not to think too much about it.

A few houses with tiny gardens and wrought-iron fences were interspersed among the businesses. A white-haired woman sat on the porch of one these houses. Dana had just convinced herself she was accomplishing nothing and that there was laundry to do at home. She turned on the sidewalk in front of the home and the white-haired lady. Dana nodded and the lady returned the greeting.

Dana stepped to the fence and put her hands on the warm metal. "Do...you have a beautiful home. Have you lived here long?"

"For five years, back from '65 to '70. We rented. My son bought it ten years ago."

"Isn't that something? He must have enjoyed living here back then."

"I guess so."

"Lots of changes in the last ten years, let alone from 1970."

The old woman chuckled and waved a thin hand in Dana's direction. "What're you talking about? Bad thing is, they put up a new building or tear a house down and in no time you forget what the street used to look like. It fades away."

Just then there was a bump at her front door. But the old lady expected it and turned and opened the screen. A steel-colored walker came out first and she put one hand on it while still holding the door open. A man whose hair was every bit as white as hers stepped behind the walker.

She said something to him and he replied, "Is that right?"

Dana had wanted to ask her if she saw many homeless in the area. She felt embarrassed to ask.

"Are you looking for someplace in particular?" the woman asked. "Bob's the one good with directions. Aren't you, Bob?" She held the door for him until he and the walker cleared the doorway. Once she let go of the door, she placed a hand to his back. Dana saw a wealth of affection in the woman's touch, like she was steadying him and caressing him at the same time with that frail hand. Dana knew they were a married couple, not brother and sister, or friends. She knew they'd gone through a lot together and the bond had survived. It was plain to see.

"No. Thank you. I was just, just walking and looking."

"Well," Bob said, apparently having prepared himself to dispense directions. "That's 28 North right here. A block over is 28 South. It divides into one-way streets through town."

"Yes, okay," Dana said.

There was a time, when she was newly married to Warren Reynolds, that she thought they might grow old like that. And it wasn't because of their passion for each other, which they had and which was wonderful. It was because of how easy it was to be with him, how effortlessly they had come together.

Things had moved so slowly, she had wondered if they were becoming just friends. If one counted the different times they went out together in groups, he did not try to kiss her until their fifth date, and that was three months after they had met at that pool party. But it only seemed a long wait in retrospect. All the while he had struck her as sexy, that smile and those shoulders and the way, back then, he always seemed so at ease and unflappable. That first kiss, when it came, was a long one. They were at his car. He had come over to her side to let her in. They had just had some late-night sushi after seeing a movie. She knew the kiss must be coming, and anticipated kissing him goodnight at her apartment door. But he turned her shoulders and pinned her to the side of the car. It was a dark parking lot and Dana had not seen anyone else around, but she felt uncomfortable with the public display. Later, he would say it was the sexiest move anyone had ever put on him, but it had been an accident. She had brought her hands up to his chest to push him gently away, but they lighted on his nipples. She felt them through his shirt and the kiss grew more intense. She felt his muscles quiver under her hands.

He once whispered in her ear, "I used to be afraid I'd never find you." When had Reynolds said that to her? She remembered it had come out of the blue, not on a special occasion or during a particularly romantic interlude. She had been over at his apartment on a quiet Sunday afternoon. Was it before they were engaged? He had squeezed her hand and said it.

Recalling that line now stopped her short.

A bench and a table on the old couple's porch were crowded with potted flowers. The couple was getting down to the business of watering them all. They had forgotten about Dana. She waved limply anyway and started back toward her car.

She sat in her car, swung her legs in, then swung them back out. She set off walking again, this time in the opposite direction.

She decided to see if she couldn't find that woman again—Jessie, the homeless woman who seemed to know Reynolds. The first time Dana had seen Jessie, the woman was crying and looked pathetic. She had thrown a pocketful of money in disgust. But Dana had shown her Reynolds's picture and she had said she knew him, had seen him around.

Dana wore a pair of flats and had not planned on this much walking. Her feet were beginning to rebel with each uncushioned step on hard concrete. She returned to the gas station where she and Jessie had met. She was conscious not to look as if she were just hanging around since the manager had already shooed her away once before. Dana crossed the street, passed a Vietnamese restaurant, and turned into a lot that had once been a Hess gas station. The pumps had been removed. Tall weeds grew from cracks in the pavement. Dana recalled buying gas here one October during the terror reign of the DC sniper. She had inserted the nozzle quickly, then hunkered down on the far side of the car, letting it shield her from the pumps and the traffic, feeling particularly stupid the whole time. Two of the sniper's victims had been in this area. Once, while going into a Giant grocery, she had seen a man emerge with his groceries and start walking in a brisk zigzag pattern. Everyone nearby who saw him knew immediately what he was doing and they all laughed nervously. Behind the little gas station building was an abandoned garage. Dana was surprised to see a car sandwiched between the two buildings, a blue Toyota with a banged-up front bumper. The trunk was open. No one was inside, but the car was shaking with a rhythm.

The empty car's movement froze Dana.

She heard a grunt and then another. Dana took a step back. Her first thought was that someone had been put in the trunk of the car and had managed to pop it open and was trying to climb out. She fished her cell phone from her purse. It seemed to take an inordinately long time to locate it. Her thumb hovered over the phone. She was aware that she was invisible from the road and the intersection. "Hello?" she asked.

She stepped past the hood of the car to the rearview mirror. The car was still shivering, seemingly of its own accord. Then she thought to take a wider approach. She stepped away with her thumb still hovering over the nine. "Hello?"

She took another big step to the side nearer the back wall of the Hess. She saw Jessie, bent over the back of the trunk, gripped from behind by a bald, red-faced man, who looked on the verge of exploding from the top of his shiny head. He had an arm around her waist and a hand gripping her shoulder. Their pants were around their ankles.

"Omigod!" Dana said.

Jessie looked up and around the raised trunk lid.

Dana stepped back, averting her face.

"Hey! Wait up. I've been looking all over for you; I know where your man is."

Dana didn't know what to do. She backed farther away. She whispered, "Maybe I should come back later?"

The grunting was louder now. The man's heavy hog-rutting snorts were answered by Jessie's lighter squealed replies. Even with the cell phone in one hand, Dana covered her nose and mouth in a cup of her hands.

The car stopped shaking.

After a couple of seconds, the man said, "Watch your hands. Watch your hands, God damn it." The trunk was suddenly slammed shut.

He had pulled up his pants, but Jessie had been holding on to the car, off balance, still trying to fish hers up over her knees. She had to snatch her hands clear.

Dana and the bald man's eyes met for a fraction and he cut his away, then put up a hand as a shield, like a blinder. "God damn it," he said again.

He climbed into the car quickly. He fumbled with his keys while trying to hide his face from her. The car started and jumped forward at once, spitting pebbles and dust behind it.

Dana saw Jessie's pale, thin legs and dark patch as she struggled with her pants while squinting against the flying dust and grit.

"Hey, girl," she said, zipping her fly. "I know where that man of yours is. I take it you ain't found him yet?" She casually dusted herself off. "Yeah, I can take you to him. Got a car?" She rubbed her right shoulder, the one the man had been gripping, and grimaced.

It was her only acknowledgement that Dana hadn't just caught her chatting with a friend.

They were a block back down 28 toward Dana's car when Jessie stopped. Dana stopped three steps past her and looked back. Jessie fished into her pants pocket and pulled out crumpled bills. She looked at them without counting them or taking the effort to smooth them out. Tears fell from her eyes, but she made no sound. In a moment, she continued walking.

Jessie stank up the car again. Franklin had noticed it when he was in the car after Jessie had been in it the first time. He had crinkled his nose and said something about the funk of 40,000 years. Dana had smiled briefly. That had set her to wondering, again, if she should tell Franklin anything about who she had seen and what she was doing.

"I need a sip of a little something. Jesus, I'm frazzled today. Just out of sorts today. Can we go by a ABC first? Down this away." She pointed and Dana rolled her eyes and steered toward the liquor store.

Dana idled out front as Jessie literally ran in. She was in there for several minutes and came running out.

"I need four more dollars...five more dollars," she said, leaning in the window.

Dana thought, *You're not charging enough.* She opened her purse and handed Jessie a five.

Jessie ran back into the store.

Dana thought of her son running into his favorite comic-book shop.

Jessie scurried out seconds later with a bottle sheathed in a slim brown bag. She was already drinking from it by the time she opened the car door. She held it out for Dana, who shook her head without looking at her. "Well, it's just that it's a tiresome day. A sip. Go right up here. Back toward downtown. We'll find that man of yours. You ain't gonna give him over to the police or nothing like that, are you?"

"No. Nothing like that."

"Okay. Left."

They were back in the Old Town area.

"I don't know what I'm going to do, really."

"Oh. I do," Jessie said and took another sip from her bottle.

Dana wondered if it was illegal to have open liquor in her car. She scanned for police cars.

"You're going to welcome him back as if nothing bad ever happened. Like nobody said what everyone remembers they said. Like nobody hurt nobody. Like nobody hit nobody. And you'll make him a good meal, right? And then come later, you ain't gonna be able to help yourself and you gotta ask, 'Why'd you go?' Pull over here, hon."

Dana slid the car into a parking spot near the Old Town train station. Evening seemed to be coming faster now.

Jessie said, "Then, it won't matter what he says. If he answers ''Cause,' that will pee you off because it don't make horse sense. And if he says nothing, that will pee you too. And before the end of the day you'll all be in it again, the whole damn family shouting and spitting and no one can hear themselves think. And by sunrise he'll be gone again."

"Sounds like experience talking," Dana said, straightening from the car.

"It ain't all a bad thing. 'Cause you won't feel the need to look for him after that."

"Why's that?"

"'Cause you'll have your answer."

"What answer, Jessie?"

"That he don't know why he left anymore'n you do."

They passed a tiny park, half a block in size, with a small gazebo and a pavilion for evening bands. On the train tracks that formed the border for one side of the park was a red caboose. Dana had seen it often and never given it any thought. There were bushes on the park side of the caboose and Jessie parted the bushes slowly. Behind the bushes and beneath the caboose were palettes of cardboard used as beds, along with trash and newspaper and a very dirty blanket. There were three such places where it was obvious men slept. The greasy, flattened boxes were molded to shoulder blades and knees. The spot was smelly and dirty.

Jessie sang, "Hey, ho, nobody home. Meat nor drink nor money have I none. Hey ho, nobody home."

"He sleeps here? Outside?"

"C'mon."

Jessie led her across the tracks to the train station. At one time it was abandoned, but it had recently received a lot of love and tax dollars and now served as the town's visitor center.

Jessie made a show of looking around before signaling Dana to follow. They crossed Prince William Street to the Manassas Museum, where two Civil War-era cannons guarded the sidewalk approach to the building. Jessie veered to the trees lining one side of the building. Here too were hidden spaces where people had slept in the shadowy area formed by the trees. Someone was beneath the boxwood shrubs that grew along the brick wall of the museum. He lay fetal, knees drawn up. He was wearing jeans and had a brown jacket draped over his shoulders like a blanket.

They could hear his snoring.

Jessie put an index finger to her lips. "Wait," she whispered. She crept to the sleeping man and bent over him. She then waved Dana away and followed her. Out from under the trees, Jessie said, "It was a white man."

"I want to ask him if he's seen Reynolds." Dana pulled the photo from her purse.

"He ain't seen him. He ain't seen anything."

"I'd like to try."

"Suit yourself," Jessie said, sounding abruptly angry. She crossed her arms. "Can't let someone sleep it off."

"One second." Dana knew the woman wasn't going to leave her; she had left her bottle of "a little something" in her car.

Dana stooped and went under the low limbs.

Jessie stood in the front yard of the museum.

The man's broken snoring sounded louder. Dana had her photo out and in front of her. "Excuse me. Excuse me, sir," she said. "Sir?"

The snoring stopped, but the man didn't move. He made a sound as if he were sucking his teeth.

"Sir?"

He moved with a start, one of his hands shooting up defensively. "What is it? Go away."

"I'm sorry to wake you, sir. I'm looking for this man." She held out her photo. "Perhaps you've seen him around? Here, the man in the photo?"

"Huh? No, I ain't seen him. You have some spare change? I need to get something to eat. A sandwich. Let me see the picture again. Can't see up in here. It's too dark."

"I do have some change."

He had to struggle to stand. He walked bent in half out from under the trees. He stopped when he saw Jessie, then looked around.

"She's with me," Dana said.

His brown hair was wild and spiky. He must have spotted Dana eyeing it because he smoothed it down with his free hand.

"Huh. Now let's see." He took the picture from Dana. Still bent, he looked at it. "Don't know who he is, but, yeah, I've seen him 'round town. Over by the church kitchen, maybe." He waved a hand in front of him that seemed to encompass the entire town.

"Do you know where he sleeps? Where he stays?"

He breathed out, loudly. His tired, sagging eyes were almost painful to look at.

Dana handed him a folded ten-dollar bill, which Jessie eyed.

He took the money back under the trees without looking back.

Jessie said. "No one should be allowed to wake up a sleeping person. No good can come of it. It should be a law, like unless the building is on fire or something."

"Jessie, there's a soup kitchen around here?"

She nodded. "They ain't open today. They raise such a fuss; can't just let people be. I don't go there."

"Where is it? Let's go by."

"They only open three days a week."

Back in the car, Jessie held her bottle in her lap. Dana could see her thinking about taking a sip. Her grip tightened on the bottle, as if she were holding it down to stop it from rising to her mouth. After a few seconds, she grinned, gave Dana directions, unscrewed the cap, and took a long swallow. "What a day," she said.

Dana wondered if Reynolds was in similar condition, sleeping in dirty nooks and crannies, bewildered and boozing. If so, maybe it would be better not to find him.

Jessie wasn't sure where the soup kitchen was, though she kept acting as if she knew it was on the corner of the next block.

"Do you ever go there?" Dana asked.

"Oh, no," she said, looking out the passenger window.

This gave Dana an idea for an entirely new approach to her search. She would call the local governments and churches to find out where charities that worked with or for the homeless were located, and she would search for Reynolds in those places. She filled with a new hope.

Finally, they passed a church, and Jessie pointed, telling Dana this was the soup kitchen. They had already passed the church, a little Greek Orthodox church near the old town, at least twice before, so Dana did not pull into the parking lot with any confidence.

The lot was completely vacant and the church's doors closed. Dana hopped out to check. She almost left the car running, but at the last second and with a glance toward Jessie, she took her keys with her. None of the doors along the front or back of the sanctuary would open. There was a building in back that looked, from Dana's brief peek through a window, like a small cafeteria.

Dana got back in the car. She was sure Jessie had tipped up that bottle again.

"Let's go, Jessie," she said. "We need to do a bit of shopping."

She took almost an hour going over shoe after shoe in wildly different styles—pumps, espadrilles, strappies. Dana followed along with her, offering comments every now and then: "Cute but not too practical." Jessie finally settled on a pair of green pumps with four-inch heels.

"Jessie," Dana said. "Those are not going to be comfortable for walking the street—I mean, for walking around."

"Are the shoes for me or not?"

Dana tried waiting her out, hoping she would change her mind. Jessie left her old shoes right there on the showroom floor and walked out with a strut and a grin. Her butt rolled and there was no wobble in her step. Dana had to admit, the woman knew how to walk in heels.

VIII. SLEEK, HE SAID

Dana was trying to think. She didn't even know what she was putting in her cart half the time. She felt a flush of shame; covering her whereabouts with a quick trip to the grocery store brought back memories. People might not ask what took you so long if you came in with a couple of bags of groceries. At least you had an answer to the question.

She was preoccupied. Her principal had said, "Maybe you've reached the seven-year burnout, just four years delayed."

Looking at the items in her cart, she decided she had gotten enough. She didn't really have any need to be shopping now anyway. She made a quick U-turn and collided with another shopping cart that was coming up behind her.

"Whoa," the man with the cart said. "I thought you had stopped. I was going around."

"Oh, excuse me."

"Good thing we're not driving cars! We don't have to exchange insurance information."

"Yes." Dana made herself laugh.

"I told the management here they needed turn signals on these things. I don't think they took my suggestion too seriously."

Dana smiled, not really listening to the man. She was wondering what Maureen Reynolds was thinking at this moment. Maybe—and this would be for the best—she had not believed her former daughter-in-law when Dana told her she had seen her son. Maybe it would be best if Maureen believed only that Dana was being cruel and hurtful, and now hated her more than ever. But Maureen had invested a lot of prayers in her son's resurrection; she might already believe more in the reappearance than Dana did.

She went to check out and bought whatever it was that she had tossed in her cart.

She placed her purchases on the passenger-side seat. She noticed she had bought two large-sized boxes of Cheerios, but then remembered Franklin no longer liked them.

"Hey," she heard just as she was opening her driver's-side door. She turned to see a man in a green sweater with brown elbow patches calling to her.

It was apparently the man she'd run into with her cart, but she was really seeing him for the first time just now. He was only an inch or two taller than her, yet she could tell he was solid. He had black hair, arranged in just a bit of a comb-over. *Don't they know, it never, ever works?*

"Trying to sound kind of cool and carefree here," he said and chuckled.

Dana fixed a polite smile to her face.

"Say, if we had banged cars instead of carts that might not be so bad. At least then I might have your phone number? You know, when you have to exchange information."

Dana thought, *Didn't he just make that same joke in the store?* She was preoccupied, just like the principal had said. That reminded her: she had essays in need of grading. Holding the same smile, she nodded to the man and climbed into her car.

She joined the stream of traffic. Tomorrow she would go by the shelter. "It don't take much to be homeless. All you good church-going, tax-paying, nine-to-five citizens would be shocked to your core if you knew how thin the walls of your houses really were." Then Jessie had looked down at her pretty new shoes.

———————

The groceries hadn't been necessary. Brenda did not see her un-loading the car and Franklin was not home. It was way after seven. Dana could not account for much of the afternoon having spi-raled away. She set her bags on the kitchen counter, then jogged next door.

Brenda did not return Dana's smile. She stepped away from the doorway.

Dana followed her back to the kitchen.

Her friend's face remained flat when Dana asked her how things were going. Dana didn't know how to read the look. "How's my boy?" she asked.

"I'd be the one to ask." Brenda was unloading her dishwasher.

"What?"

"If you want to know what Franklin is up to, I am the woman to ask." Brenda's hands were on her hips. "Upstairs with my other kids."

"Brenda—"

"Never mind. I'm in a foul mood. I want to go on a real vacation this year, not watch TV with Geoff's mother for two weeks. I say Virginia Beach. You know what he says, 'Honey, she's *old*.'"

Dana told herself to call Maureen.

"Dana? You didn't hear a word I just said."

"No. I did. Pick someplace where he can golf, Brenda."

"Oh, then I'd be vacationing with just me and the kids. Next subject. Did you call the police about the prowler?"

Dana shook her head.

"Why not? You want to be on record as having made a complaint even if they do nothing about it. I'm not sending my good-for-nothing husband out there again. I love him."

Dana smiled at her friend. "Let me go take Frankie off your hands."

"Honey, I'm sorry. Truth is Franklin is no trouble at all. I wish sometimes my kids were that quiet. He's already eaten."

Dana went to the staircase and called her son.

"One minute," she heard from the floor above.

Dana returned to Brenda's kitchen and picked up a dish towel, wiped a slightly damp mug, and handed it to Brenda. "I want to tell you what's happened," she said.

Brenda froze while tiptoeing to reach the mug's shelf. "What's happened?"

Dana's throat filled. "I didn't call the cops because I think I know who was in my backyard."

"Dana, who?"

"I think it was Reynolds."

"Who's that?"

"My Reynolds. Warren Reynolds."

"Oh, Dana…"

"No, no, don't 'Oh, Dana' me like that. I saw him."

"In your backyard."

"No. Earlier."

"Honey…"

Dana looked over her shoulder and moved closer to Brenda so that only the opened door of the dishwasher was between them. "I haven't told Franklin," she whispered. "I was heading home the other day. There was a big accident and traffic was shit. But that's neither here nor there. At the light at Liberia there was a panhandler mooching during the red lights."

Brenda looked at her, eyebrows furrowed, listening.

"So, I'm like, hurry and turn green, damn it. 'Cause he was coming my way. His sign—his sign read 'Need change. Need a chance.' Which I thought was, you know, pithy. I mean, maybe it doesn't even refer to money, change. Maybe he means social change, better economic regulation, increased access to housing…"

"Dana."

"The light turns green just as he comes up to my car. I had to wait for the car in front of me to get his ass in gear. But I make it, right? And as I drive by I look right in his face."

"No!"

"It's Warren."

"No!"

"My Reynolds. Franklin's father." She looked over her shoulder again, but she could hear children's voices from the ceiling.

"You're sure? You've talked to him."

"Talked? No. I haven't seen him since. I went back. After I got over my shock, I turned around and went back to the intersection, but he was already gone."

"And that was him in the backyard?"

"I didn't get a good look."

Brenda sat down at her kitchen table, not taking her eyes off Dana. "It's been—it must have been…well, Franklin's nine years old. Nine years. Dana."

Dana sat down too.

"So he doesn't call, but he drops in and has a smoke in the middle of the night?"

"Ever since, I've been looking for him. I met this woman. I show around his photo. She recognized him, said she sees him around. She's a street person."

"I didn't think we had street people in the suburbs. Though I have seen the panhandlers at the intersections before. Dana, honey, do you think it's just wishful thinking?"

"I've always believed he was gone. Felt it, you know. Just felt the hollow of him not there, not here. I used to have a running argument with his mother. She would say, 'You cannot declare him dead without a body.' She would tell me I had to have faith. Her kind of faith, which she was sure I didn't have because I refused to go to her church. But she fought me on that, said I just wanted the insurance money."

"Yeah, I never got what the hell was wrong with wanting the insurance money. You needed it."

"Well, when the person is still alive, it starts getting kinda wrongish to want the money."

"And you haven't told Franklin?"

Dana shook her head. She reached for another plate from the dishwasher and dried it. She grabbed another.

"Don't tell him, honey. Don't dare. In fact, don't tell anybody until you're sure. No, until I'm sure. Don't tell anybody until I'm sure."

"Brenda."

"I'll tell Geoff, of course, spousal privilege and all."

"Understood."

"I'd say tell the cops. Just to let them know. If he's sneaking around here."

"No, Brenda. I want to help him." Dana thought for a minute. "Besides, if the insurance company found out I thought he was alive, they might try to get their money back plus interest. Omigod."

Brenda started shaking her head rapidly. "Then maybe you don't think you saw him, with the sign? It wasn't him."

Dana returned to drying and stacking plates. Brenda tried to pull the cloth from her hand, but Dana held it tightly. The tug-of-war was brief; Brenda let go.

She said, "Why would he disappear? He was your husband. Why would he leave you bleeding in a car halfway in the river?"

Tears started rolling down Dana's cheeks. She sniffed. "Don't get me crying. I don't want Franklin to see…"

"Warren Reynolds was a good guy, right? Why would he do that? Leave you and Franklin? He knew you were pregnant, right?"

"Yes." *And had plenty of reason to believe it wasn't his*, Dana thought. "I didn't tell you I saw him so you could tell me I didn't see him."

Franklin and Anthony and Nicole came bounding down the stairs.

Dana quickly wiped her face and eyes with the dish towel.

Franklin frowned when he saw his mother's face. He said, "Hey. I already ate."

She wears her short pencil skirt. The one she skipped two weeks' worth of lunches to afford. The one that causes the fourth-grade boys to stare after her when she walks down the hall. She is wearing her trim Nine West boots with it. She gets the compliments she hoped for.

She walks by Steve. Stick legs and knobby knees dangling from a long line of blue gym shorts follow after him. He is herding the last of his kids into the gymnasium. She turns back to look at him and he makes a great show of pretending he is not looking at her, idly whistling, and gazing at nothing just above his head. He then looks directly at her with a smile so wide its meaning is unmistakable. He is a flirt. She is warmed. She thinks she hears him say, "Sleek."

Steve is good with the kids. He can talk Xbox and Pokémon and Sith Lords with any of them. He wears his cap backwards, has a full head of blond hair, and is clean shaven. He has small lips and what's almost a cleft in his chin. He can talk to the kids, Dana concludes, because he isn't much removed from being one himself.

He makes sure to sit next to her or across from her in meetings.

Sometime after the beginning of the new school year, he begins to touch her. The contact is nothing inappropriate. He will put a finger to her elbow or rest a hand on her shoulder. She never thinks much of it. It is innocuous.

He flatters her. Sometimes he says a bit too much and she has to scold him. He pouts and she laughs and waves him away while shaking her head.

They end up on the science fair committee together and work after hours, when the school is an empty maze of echo chambers. They judge the volcanoes and solar systems and ant farms together. He makes her laugh and she wonders why it seems being around him is easier than being around Warren.

She is putting math problems on the board for tomorrow's class on long division. She can hear a few kids squealing and laughing outside her class windows.

She hears someone enter her room, but she doesn't turn around. She continues to put numbers on the board.

Steve clears his throat and says, "I have a petition here signed by the vast majority of the fourth, fifth, and sixth grade boys of Oak Lane Elementary demanding you wear that skirt at least twice a week."

She turns momentarily, sees his smile. "It's not unprofessional is it? Any faculty talking? The hemline is just above—"

"No," he says quickly. "It's just that you wear the shit out of it."

"Listen to you."

"No, you listen to me."

He puts his hands to her waist. She's amazed she didn't sense him getting that close to her. He nuzzles her neck.

"Okay, mister," she says in the classroom voice she uses on her students.

She turns on him, but he does not step back. His face is an inch from hers. "Steve," she says. "Please."

"No."

That first kiss sends her heart racing. She is shocked and wants to shock him, too. She thinks at first this is a part of their game. Her heart races. The chalk falls to the floor and breaks. He steps back. His tongue licks his bottom lip. His eyes are big.

"I didn't get the door," he says. He points to the windows. "Get the blinds."

"Hey, wait a second."

"Get the blinds." He looks both ways down the hallway, then closes the door. Dana heads across the classroom toward the windows.

Her only advance warning about this moment, or the ramifications of this moment, had come days before. Steve and Dana and a handful of others were in the faculty lounge. They were laughing at something a student had done in the cafeteria. She doesn't remember the story, but they were all laughing and Steve had put a hand to that spot between her neck and shoulder and squeezed quickly before taking it away. Only one person had noticed. Mrs. Thurman, one of the older teachers nearing retirement, had given Dana a look—the same stern gaze, Dana was sure, she had used to upbraid unruly students for years. Dana had not fully understood at first, but dwelled on it the rest of the day.

Dana had sent Franklin out back to shake out a few rugs. He returned, calling her, loosening her from the past.

"Mom, are you smoking?"

"Huh? No, honey."

"You could get lung cancer or emphysema. And it's stinky besides."

"What brought on this health lesson?"

"I was just on the patio. There's all these cigarette butts out there. Like six of them."

A banging at the front door made them both jump. They looked at each other.

"Who's that?" Franklin went around Dana.

She recovered in time to catch him by the bottom of his T-shirt. "No, baby. Let me get it."

The banging continued.

"Dang," said Franklin. "They're going to beat the door down."

Dana was still chilled by Franklin's discovery. Her front door vibrated under the pounding.

By standing as far to the right of her front window as she could, she tried to see who was at the door. It only worked if the person took a step or two back after knocking. Dana put the chain on the door and looked back at Franklin, who looked braced though he was still holding the bathroom rugs.

She opened the door.

No, it was not Reynolds, but the resemblance was uncanny. It was Ness. Her eyebrows dipped over her brown eyes and her lips were turned up in a teeth-baring snarl. "Let me in."

Dana took a second and Ness repeated her demand. Dana said, "I don't think I want to."

"Who is it?" Franklin was asking behind her.

"Frankie, is that you, hon?"

"Hey, Aunt Nessie." Franklin came forward.

"Hey, babe. Let me in so I can beat the white off your mama."

Franklin giggled until he saw the look on his aunt's face. "What's wrong?" he asked.

"Dana!"

Maureen must have finally told her daughter of their visit and of how it ended. Dana had always been a little afraid of her sister-in-law. Reynolds said they used to get in fights when they were younger and Nessie had won all of them except the last one. He said he had stopped fighting her when he realized he could win.

"Frankie, the womenfolk have to talk. Let me in and then run on upstairs."

Dana held up a finger. She tried to close the door, but Ness had her foot wedged in the opening. Dana gave her a look and she moved it. "You go over to Brenda's," she told her son. He questioned her with a look and she said she would be all right, though she wasn't sure.

Dana unlatched the chain and opened the door and Ness pushed by both of them. She tried to look calm for Franklin's sake.

Dana held the door open for him.

He shook his head.

"Franklin."

He crossed his arms.

"Frankie, give us a minute. Then I want to come say hey. Okay?"

"If you promise not to fight."

"Frankie—"

"Just promise."

She did. He made his mother promise too. He picked up the rugs from where he'd dropped them and set them on the landing to the stairs. He went outside, looking back at both of them.

Dana was ready. She was no fighter, but she could scratch and bite as well as anyone and was not going to hesitate to do so.

Ness held up an index finger and wagged it at Dana. It was then Dana noticed the tears welling in her sister-in-law's eyes.

"I warned my brother about you. And this was after I got to know you a bit. I said, she's not serious, Warren. I told him you wanted everything to be like you were still in college or high school. I warned him. God damn me if I didn't warn him. Bitch. Bitch!"

"I'm the bitch? I didn't come over to your place and try to beat your door down and scare your kid, if you had one, bitch!"

"No, you went to my mama's house and you told that old woman who's dying of cancer...dying of *cancer*...that her dead son is still alive!" Ness was livid. She was trembling.

Dana thought, *the wig. That ugly, plastic wig.*

"She don't know what to think anymore. Why would you say something like that? You done punched her in the gut."

"No."

"She pissed you off because she wants to see her own grandson, so you thought you'd kick her while she's down?" The words and spit flew from Ness's mouth.

"Nessie, stop."

Her watery eyes did not drop a tear, but Ness trembled with rage. Her hands were knotted in front of her, moving about as if she didn't know what to do with them. "Thank God, Frankie made me promise. Mama don't know what to think anymore. I think she's taken a downturn. I think you got her good. She's confused. Hell, I'm confused. Why did you say that to her?"

Dana looked away. She saw the pile of throw rugs where Franklin had left them, but couldn't remember why they were there. "I...I told her to hurt her."

"*What?*"

"I didn't know she was sick. I'm sorry."

Nessie crossed the short distance between them as quick as snapping fingers. "I'm more than sorry Reynolds ever married you. I'm just so, ugh! I'm just so sorry you're the one raising my nephew. God damn it." She pushed Dana's hand from the doorknob and opened it. "I'm going to be bringing Mama up here from time to time to see Frankie and you better not do one thing to get in our way," she said. Then she was gone.

Dana followed her out a few steps.

Nessie stormed down the sidewalk. Brenda emerged, jogging over from next door while holding a hand out to Franklin to stay put. Franklin was standing in Brenda's doorway.

Dana said in as even a voice as she could, "But Ness, I wasn't lying."

Nessie stopped so quickly, it was as if Dana could hear tires squealing.

"Hi, Nessie. How are you?"

Ness turned slowly. She looked back at Dana. "Hey, Brenda," she said without taking her eyes from Dana.

"She told me yesterday. C'mon back inside."

Brenda climbed the steps. After a handful of seconds, Ness followed.

"Franklin said y'all were about to fight. I told him I'd come over and referee."

"You *saw* Warren?" Nessie sat on the arm of Dana's recliner. Brenda sat in the recliner. The two women did not know each other well, but had spoken on rare occasions.

Dana breathed out. "You don't have to believe me. It's okay. I didn't expect anyone to believe me. That's why I wasn't going to tell."

"She told my mother this shit. Mom's sick. Undergoing daily chemo and radiation."

Brenda said, "I'm sorry."

"I said I'm sorry. And I am too, Nessie. I didn't know about Maureen. I was just in a crappy mood that day. But I saw Warren, and now I'm trying to find him again."

"I don't understand. What did he say? Where has he been?"

"I haven't talked to him yet."

"Tell her."

"I saw him on the curb as I was driving by."

"Aw, shit." Nessie waved her away.

"I got a good look! He was closer to me than you are now. I know what my own husband looks like, thank you. He has the same forehead, the bridge of his nose, the way it tapers, it's the same as yours, Nessie. It was Warren." Dana proceeded to repeat the story of the intersection. His sign, his clothes, his shaggy, scraggly appearance. How she had looked him in the eye. She said she had even met a woman who recognized him.

Nessie had a hand covering her mouth.

Brenda kept looking at her, reading her reactions, Dana supposed. Brenda seemed to be enjoying this, Dana realized, and that was starting to piss Dana off.

"You moved. But Mom hasn't. Me neither. Why hasn't he been by to see us?"

Dana shrugged.

"Why would he be panhandling? And why around here?"

Dana shook her head.

"If this was a soap opera," Brenda said, "then, of course, we would know he has amnesia and doesn't remember who he is or where he lived. And his wallet came out of his pocket so he couldn't look at the address on his driver's license or check the name on his MasterCard."

Dana wiped her eyes. Her fingers came away wet. "I don't need either of you to believe me. I know he's alive."

"You're the one who had him declared dead."

"I saw him. I've been trying to find him ever since. I've been driving around...he's out there. He's out there in the night, sleeping under trains, in back alleys, standing on streets begging for money. I have to find him. I have to bring him back. He's my son's father. He was a good, good man. Choose not to believe me, Nessie. I don't care. I don't need you to believe me. He is out there and I think he's trying to find his way home. I really think he is. Something's stopping him. He can't quite get by it. But he...I need to find him."

Dana stood in front of her sister-in-law and neighbor, drops falling from her nose. She felt more certain than ever that Reynolds was alive, and in the same town. She was convinced—eventually, she would find him.

Brenda said, "Nessie, did your brother smoke?"

"No, why?"

Brenda looked at Dana.

Dana said, "He didn't stand on street corners before, either."

Nessie stood. "Brenda, you want to know what happened with that car crash? From what I could figure out, your girl here was fussin' with my brother while they were in his car at night in the rain. She distracted him."

"Nessie."

"You told me once way back y'all were having an argument that night. He lost control and skidded down an embankment. They both survived, but were banged up and part of the car was in the river. He got out and went around to get Dana out. But he was still woozy, maybe he'd hit his head. Going around the car, he fell in the river. Maybe he passed out. And, um, the currents took him away."

Ness had never come right out and said that to her before. Dana had long suspected Warren's family blamed her. She never knew to what extent. "Brenda, she doesn't know that. I was there and I don't know what happened. Not for sure," Dana said.

"You haven't told Frankie?"

"No."

Nessie turned to Brenda. "May I go over your place and visit my nephew?"

"Sure."

She left without looking back at Dana.

"Let's get you some coffee," Brenda said. She wrapped her arms about Dana and gave her a hug. It felt good.

"You weren't much help."

"I came to see a fight. Imagine my disappointment."

"Must suck."

"She believed you, sweetie. I watched her face. You scared the bejeezus out of her."

IX. MATH AND CONSEQUENCES

There's talk. Dana wonders what they know and wonders what they speculate. She catches certain looks before her friends and co-workers cut their eyes away or force on their smiles. There's sympathy from some of those looks, which makes her feel burdened and heavier than the extra pounds she's gained, and from a few there is amusement, or accusation.

The baby shower is subdued and perfunctory. The manners of a grade-school faculty require that there be a shower. All the big milestones have to be acknowledged and celebrated and organized as an assembly. It isn't a party Dana wants. But she needs the gifts she registered for: the bassinet, the creams, the bottles, the diaper hamper, the car seat.

Her sister-in-law, Ness Macklin, was appointed co-host by Dana's co-workers and she is dutifully clearing away the torn wrapping paper and abandoned plates of partially eaten cake. Dana actually experiences a cold shiver when she wonders if Maureen and Ness should be here at all.

Someone asks her if she is okay.

"A kick," she answers. That answer, apparently, invites another hand to her stomach.

Dana has decided to move. The For Sale sign is out front. She loves the house, but cannot afford it with Reynolds gone. She hopes it doesn't take long to sell.

Her friends are generous. She has everything she needs in order to start her new life with this child. They *ooh* and *ahh* over each little outfit, blanket, and toy. She has been to many of these events for some of the same women in the room. They have been more generous with her, she thinks. The widow.

The awkwardness doesn't go away until the last guest leaves.

Steve comes by. He knocks just minutes after everyone has left and Dana thinks he must have been sitting out there waiting. She hopes no one saw him. She looks around him for witnesses. This causes him to look over his shoulder.

"I waited until they were all gone," he says.

She lets him in.

They haven't spoken in a while. She finds she resents him at this moment. She wants to blame him for a lot of what has happened— her swollen feet and engorged breasts, but also for the car accident, for Reynolds's last words, for her widowhood.

He is looking around at all the colorful, brand-new items cluttering the living-room floor.

"I told Anne."

"There was no reason to." She is not surprised that he has confessed, now that she thinks about it. His wife has friends on the faculty and staff and that explains the looks.

"I'm not the type who can live with the guilt," he says as if this is a mark of a morally superior conscience.

He is still wearing his ball cap backwards. She decides at that moment that no one over 12 should wear his cap backwards. Punks.

He's talking, but she is not hearing it all. Anne is leaving for Wisconsin, where her mother and sisters live. He asks if she knows if it's a boy or a girl.

Now she knows what he wants to know.

He is looking amongst the blankets and jumpers for clues, but black babies and white babies use the same color blankets. "What are you going to do?"

"What?"

"About Anne leaving. What are you going to do?"

He shakes his head. "Don't know. I might go with her. I think she might take me back if I go with her. Don't know." He looks at her then, as if inviting her to say something.

"You still look good," he says when she says nothing.

"I'm so tired these days." Dana puts her hand on the doorknob.

He steps close at an angle in order to get his face close to hers. She leans backward and puts a hand up between them just in time. She feels his lips brush her palm.

She is having Warren Reynolds declared dead. How many times can she betray the same man?

When she opens the door, he walks through it, but he pauses. "It doesn't have to be like this, does it?"

As she closes the door, she is thinking, *we were careful*. She remembers being careful. She remembers back and performs some quick period math. She looks down at the hard mound hitched to her. *That was not your father. Do you hear me? Pay attention; there will be a test. That was not your father.*

She wasn't a widow any longer, she had just realized. And her marriage was now 12 years old. She was simply an abandoned wife and mother, a figure for whom the world felt less sympathy.

Murmuring started. Mrs. Reynolds's fourth-grade class could see more buses pulling up. Several buses had been lining up for a while, so emancipation was near. Dana saw the distracted boys looking up from their opened books toward the windows or the clock. She said nothing. The kids were restless. Even her best students had glazed, unreceptive eyes, while others passed messages or game cards or doodles of naughty pictures.

She was grading papers on their time, waiting for her concentration to kick in. The bell rang. Twenty-four faces looked up toward her at once. "Make certain you finish your reading tonight. Go."

High-pitched voices, scooting chairs, and the classroom was efficiently emptied in seconds.

She had already forgotten about the stack of papers on her desk and the Excel spreadsheet on her laptop. Her laptop monitor timed out without her noticing. She had decided to check the homeless shelter Jessie had mentioned and maybe the back of the museum too, though she was uncomfortable with the thought of going back down there, behind the bushes, alone.

It was so odd to her that humans could slip into such small cracks and crannies, that a whole human person could be tucked away under our noses, out of sight and mind.

Dana heard the running footsteps and from experience knew they were aimed at her classroom door. She looked up to see Gregory Bingham in the doorway.

"What did you forget, Gregory?"

He did not answer. His eyes cut to the hallway. Dana heard another set of footsteps. A woman stepped into the classroom. She was heavy breasted, with eyebrows badly in need of trimming. Her facial features and Gregory's had little resemblance. She was older than most of Dana's mothers.

Gregory hung back. He was still near the door, ready to bolt.

"We talked on the phone two weeks ago," the woman said. She had a math test in her hands. Dana could see the red F in her own handwriting. "I'm sorry, I'm Karen. I'm Greg's mom. We spoke on the phone?"

"Yes." Dana half stood and shook Mrs. Bingham's hand.

Then came the sinking feeling as her slow-working brain divined why Gregory Bingham's mother was here. Instead of sitting back down, Dana skirted her desk and sat at a student's desk and motioned for Mrs. Bingham to take one. The woman looked at the small seat and opted to lean against Dana's desk.

Dana was trying to think. She remembered the phone call now. Mrs. Bingham was upset about her son's math work. She might have told this woman she was giving Gregory extra work and a bit of after-class support. How had they left it?

"I won't keep you, but I found this in Greg's backpack." She waved the math test in Gregory's direction.

He was sitting at his desk now, two rows away.

"It shows he hasn't learned a thing. And like you say here, he's not showing how he solved any of the problems." She turned to Gregory. "I told you, you have to show your work."

"Mrs. Bingham…"

"I asked him if he'd been doing the extra assignments you've been giving him. And he's like, what extra assignments?"

"Mrs. Bingham…"

"I'm going to put him in time-out so long his baby sisters will have to visit him there when they come home from college."

"I haven't been able to work with Gregory yet."

Mrs. Bingham stopped.

"See!" Gregory Bingham stood. Obviously, he could feel his reprieve.

"They've given us twenty-seven kids apiece this year rather than have five fourth-grade classes—"

Mrs. Bingham pushed away from Dana's desk, her arms crossed. "Ms. Reynolds, I could have made other arrangements."

"I understand. We can still—"

"I could have hired a tutor. You gave him another F? You said he'd get some extra help."

Gregory's eyes were wide.

Mrs. Bingham said, "Greg, go to the stairs or the front door and wait for me there. Go."

The boy shouldered his backpack and walked out quietly.

Mrs. Bingham threw her hands up and let them fall to her lap. "Well, I'm disappointed. And here I thought he wasn't doing the extra work."

"I'm sorry."

"Okay. I understand the class-size thing, but you're the one who said you'd help out. You said it. Greg has two little sisters…I depended on you to do what you said you would—never mind. That was my mistake."

Dana stood, feeling too much like a reprimanded grade-schooler herself in the little desk.

"I apologize, Mrs. Bingham. I'll do what I can on my end to help Gregory with his math. I think mostly it's the long division."

Mrs. Bingham walked to the door shaking her head.

Dana tried to recall their phone conversation. Maybe she had made a commitment just to get Mrs. Bingham off the phone. She also wondered if this would get to her principal. The boy wasn't brilliant, but with effort he could put himself in the middle of the pack. *He deserves more help,* Dana thought. *We all do.*

⚡. EXCUSE ME, AREN'T YOU MY HUSBAND?

After swim class, Dana took her chlorine-smelling son to his favorite store, a comic-book shop called Panels that had a big sign over the entrance with a drawing of Batman on one side and Wolverine on the other.

Dana had been inside only once herself. It was a bookwormish little world, completely male.

"I thought they were supposed to be good guys," she said to him, indicating the sign. "They look menacing."

Franklin had a way of looking at her these days as if he were judging her, weighing what she said and exposing it as nonsense. He examined; there was nothing unconditional about him anymore. He was not going to take her words as law or wisdom. When it came to his mother, Dana suspected, Franklin was unconvinced.

"Mom," Franklin said, "they have to be able to scare the bad guys. Besides, nobody is all good."

"That's very true. You remember that. Can I pick you up in an hour?"

He looked surprised. Usually she waited in the car for him. "Yeah, sure." He shrugged.

"Just stay in the store until I get back."

She still had not told him about having spotted his father holding up a sign, panhandling; she doubted he would believe her anyway. Nor had she told him about the intruder in the backyard. But someone had snuck as near to them as their own patio, with just a glass door between him and them while they slept; that was a different matter. And judging by the number of butts Franklin found, it wasn't a one-time occurrence. Franklin should be placed on his guard, told to be wary, told to look out for…what, suspicious smokers? But she didn't want him to go around frightened, either. Besides, could she tell him about the intruder without telling him who she thought that intruder was? So she decided to say nothing.

With her hour, she met up with Jessie and drove over to Serve Incorporated. Jessie had told her about this family homeless shelter and soup kitchen on Dean Drive. That piece of information had cost her another twenty. That exchange was particularly stupid because she could have looked the shelter up on the Internet.

Meeting up with Jessie had almost become routine. She would find her at the gas station where they had first met. Jessie knew the times of day Dana was likely to cruise by. She would say, "Damn, if you were only here yesterday…I saw him on Center Street. Talked to him, too."

"Did you tell him I was looking for him?"

"You want him to know?" she asked.

"What did you two talk about?"

"We just said hey."

They went by Serve and Jessie got a meal.

Dana had helped out there one night, for some reason positive that Reynolds would walk in and pick up a tray. Every time the door opened, she would be looking. Mostly, though, it had been families coming in for emergency shelter, the emergencies being mostly financial.

That night, the motion-sensor light Dana had bought (and Geoff had installed over the back door, aimed at the patio) came on. She had asked the store clerk if a bird or a squirrel could cause it to turn on and he admitted they might. She could stand up on her bed and look straight down from one of her bedroom windows and see the empty patio.

She grew more frightened rather than less as the days slowly turned. She started at sounds. She jumped when Franklin would

enter the room and turn on the TV. She seemed to see dart-
ing movement peripherally and nothing at all when she turned
toward it.

She tried to estimate how much money she had given Jessie over
the past three weeks and figured it was about $200, maybe a little
more. It was money Dana could not afford. It made the difference
between when she was able to pay a bill or not, or what kind of
groceries she could purchase. And she knew the woman was probably stringing her along, grifting more money from Dana than she
earned rocking the backs of cars. But Dana still handed her the
money and bought her the meals, and even some clothes, passing
them along almost gladly and working hard at not questioning
what was happening.

After she'd dropped Franklin at the comic-book shop and
picked up Jessie, they drove by the usual places. "Do you think
he went into DC?" Dana asked again. She had asked that question
several times.

"Naw, I tol' you I just saw him the other night, remember?"

Jessie was able to get one of the last brown-bag lunches at Serve.
It was a tuna-salad sandwich, an apple, a cookie wrapped in cling
wrap, and a juice box.

"You didn't have to get that. I would have bought you something," Dana said. She only said that because her companion inspected the sandwich after every bite, curling up a lip in distaste,
only to take another bite. In the end, she ate two-thirds of it. She
ate the cookie and drained the juice box.

Dana sat next to her, but mostly didn't look her way.

Jessie had never bothered to get married herself, Dana knew,
but she did have a son. He would be an adult by now, she had once
told Dana. She had taken care of him, mostly by herself, for five or
so years, but then the father's parents had practically kidnapped
him. "They were hoity toity," she said. On the night they took him,
she had been sleeping on the couch in front of the TV and the next
thing she knew they were standing over her. The man was talking
to her. The woman was telling him what to say. And all the while,

Jessie was trying to figure out how the hell they had gotten into her apartment. The man had finally stalked off toward the boy's room and the woman just stood over her, arms crossed like she had been appointed guard duty.

"They had caught me when I wasn't feelin' too spry." Jessie said she asked the woman to get out of the way because she was blocking the television. And then she told Dana that had been a stupid thing to say, given the circumstances, and that it has been used against her in court and every day up to this very minute ever since.

She said she didn't know what was going on until the man came back with Carl sleeping on his shoulder and dragging a white plastic bag of the boy's clothes and toys.

Only then did she also see that they had some man with them, some tough in a burgundy leather jacket standing by the door. She said the only reason she saw him was because he moved forward a step or two when she made to get up from the couch.

"You can try to fight this in court," her ex-boyfriend's father had said. The side of her boy's face was molded to the man's shoulder. His mouth was open. He was asleep. "Frankly, we'd welcome that."

Jessie told Dana, "That was the last time I saw him as a little boy."

Lunch hour was long since ended and Jessie and Dana were the only ones in the little dining room. Most chairs were upside down on top of the tables. A man came in, dressed in coveralls, and rolled a bucket on wheels into the room, then left.

Dana avoided Jessie's face. How could you be so drunk you let people just walk into your place and take your child from you? Jessie had told the story without emotion, like it was just another one of the stories she was always telling. Dana never doubted that any of them were true—except the ones having to do with Reynolds.

Serve was not what she had expected. She had envisioned a storefront soup kitchen, maybe an old town house downtown, but Serve looked like a sprawling ranch structure, sunny yellow with white columns, three houses with high roofs joined together. It wasn't far away, but it was out of the way. You reached it only after a mile down a narrow, unlined road, a road without a shoulder, unsafe to walk, especially at night. It was a place you would never find if you weren't looking for it. Dana figured it was all intentional.

Dana squeezed Jessie's shoulder. The woman was bonier than she expected.

Jessie was about to respond. She smiled, but something caught her attention out the window, where they had a view of the front parking lot and, across the street, the Prince William Animal Shelter. Three people were crossing the lot.

"C'mon," Jessie said and got to her feet quickly.

"What?" Dana asked, looking out the window. She had to jog to catch up with Jessie.

"You gonna owe me," Jessie said.

"Is it—is it him? You see him?"

"See, I tol' you, gal. Tol' you…"

They hurried down a darkened hall, where the front doors waited at the end, bright rectangles of light. Dana slowed down. Jessie pushed the doors open.

Dana stepped past her a step or two and stopped.

The three people, all black, whom she had seen crossing the parking lot now stood twenty feet away.

She had never envisioned this reunion with other people present. She had found her husband. He had his back turned to her, standing with another man and a woman, listening; the woman was talking. Dana opened her mouth and raised a hand, but could generate no speech. The back of his head was a tangle of hair, flattened still from sleeping. His coat look molded to him, as if it never came off, with seams split at the joints, shiny with wear in places and soiled. It had an eight-inch rent over the right shoulder blade that exposed dirty insulation. The hems of his pant legs were frayed.

She was trying to decide what to do, but her mind refused to think properly.

His height seemed just right, as did the width of his shoulders. The proportions seemed familiar, his legs, his torso.

Her feet would not move. She would have to call out to him, get him to turn around. Once he turned around, she would know everything. She would know this was Reynolds. She would know that there were second chances. She would know Maureen was right, that you needed faith even in the face of the impossible. She would know that, eventually, Franklin would have a father. That Reynolds was alive. That she had the chance to tell him all the things she, as a widow, had so fervently wished she could tell him. And she would have the relief of knowing she had not killed him.

Her right hand was raised to the level of her face. *Excuse me, but aren't you my husband?* A tear popped from her eye. She wiped it away quickly.

She turned to her left seeking Jessie, wanting the woman with her. Jessie was gone.

"Reynolds," she said.

Jessie must have retreated back through the building.

His head and shoulders turned. He saw Dana, then looked back at his companions. They were looking at her now and he turned completely about to face her.

Since spotting the panhandler with his sign that dark evening, Dana had fantasized about this moment. The surprise on his face, first; then he would break down, sobbing, and she would console him. In a rush of words, he would explain why he had not returned to her, why he had abandoned her at the crash site. The complete amnesia. His identification swept away by the river current. They would cry together. There were variations, but essentially the scenarios had the same elements. It was her own reaction that she had not anticipated. She never expected to be face to face with the man she'd seen on the median and still not be sure that he was Warren Reynolds, her husband, the father of her son.

She was trying to say something, anything.

He said, "Did you want somebody?"

The voice sounded right, she thought. His voice got her mind to working again. She was shocked by how much her memory had abandoned her. The color of his eyes was right, the light brown chestnut color. They were looking right at her. She was stepping closer without realizing it.

"Warren, it's me, Dana."

"Dana."

There was no recognition in those chestnut eyes that she felt were so familiar. They were not looking at a wife or anyone they knew, and that stopped her from getting any closer to him. She looked up. Yes, the height was right too.

She was trying to put the eyes and the voice and the face together. She was trying to remember. It was not only her faulty memory she was dealing with, but the irrevocable changes that nearly a decade had wrought. Ten years of normal living can change your face and hair, your weight, and even your height. But ten years of living as the man in front of her may have lived, from place to place, exposed, on the street perhaps…well, she could only imagine the changes that could be wrought.

The other man said, "You should have seen her just five, ten years ago. Really. Her hair was long. Hell, now mine is longer. She don't know how to keep herself up. Damn, girl, have some pride, you know? That's what I tell her. Use to be a head turner. Men would snap they' neck as she waltzed by them."

Dana was briefly confused. It was as if her mind had been read, but apparently he was continuing a conversation they had been in earlier.

The woman said, "I lived in Raleigh back then…my own apartment."

Reynolds, the man Dana was starting to convince herself really was Warren Reynolds, did not look at either of his companions, but kept his focus on Dana.

"Nicest ass…it done fall down now. Head turner."

"Okay," this Warren said.

The woman grinned, Dana supposed, at the compliments her former self was collecting. The woman rapidly nodded.

"Titties too."

"All right," this Warren said without looking at the man.

"Head turner. Let herself go though."

"Yeah, I used to be hot," the woman said and touched her chest. She looked at the man. "Which is much better than never hot ever."

"Whoa! Hah!" This Warren Reynolds turned away then and laughed loudly.

The woman laughed too. She and Reynolds bent over as if doubled with laughter and slapped hands.

The other man watched, a bit chastened.

Dana watched Reynolds laugh. The way his mouth opened, his teeth, the way he threw his head back. His face looked younger at that moment and invoked a memory of him laughing at home, at a story she had told him about a co-worker while they were taking off their clothes in the bedroom at the end of a day. A fresh, 11-year-old memory not recalled before that moment. She compared the man she saw in front of her now to that image. Warren Reynolds.

"I got to go," the man said.

At least the other man and Dana agreed on one thing: the wide-ranging effects of ten years on the human body.

"I got to go," he said again and Reynolds and the woman finally let their laughter sniff away.

The woman wiped her eyes.

"You comin'?"

Reynolds was as scruffy as if she had found him in the Ugandan jungles or the Australian outback.

Warren Reynolds shook his head almost imperceptibly at the man.

Never once acknowledging Dana, the other man shrugged and started off.

The woman hesitated.

"I'll find y'all," Reynolds told her.

Y'all. Reynolds never said that word.

The woman nodded to Dana. She had an amused expression, which Dana thought was directed at her. She sprinted to the retreating man, hooked a finger in one of his back belt loops, and allowed herself to be towed away.

He said, "It's been a long time."

Dana felt herself breaking down, felt her muscles wavering in her chest and in her legs. Her vision blurred. "Reynolds!" she said. She closed the distance between them and hugged him around his ribs, pinning one arm. His clothes smelled. She was shaking. She told herself not to let go.

She felt his free hand on her back. She began crying.

"Okay," she heard him say. "Okay."

But it wasn't okay. She felt such a tumble of emotions she couldn't sort them all out. She was mad at him and relieved and scared and guilty and perplexed. To let her think he was dead all these years, to let her raise their son alone…

Franklin! She had left him at the strip mall, at the comic book store and that had been—she pushed away from Reynolds and checked her watch—two hours and change ago.

"I have to go," she said.

He just looked at her.

"My son, I was supposed to pick him up over an hour ago." She looked about and located her car. She also looked about for Jessie, but she was nowhere to be seen. "Damn! I have to go."

"All right, go get your boy."

"Will you be here?"

He shrugged.

What did that mean? "Do you stay here?"

"No."

"It took forever to find you. Come with me. Come with me, please?" She took one of his hands when he didn't move. It felt bold to do so, more bold than hugging him. The hand was big and rough and the nails too long. "Please?"

"Sure."

She led him to her car. They didn't say anything else. It was surreal. Now it was like a fantasy, like the fantasies a pregnant and newly widowed Dana had dreamed to life while lying across her bed in her awful loneliness.

She kept looking at him. She divided her attention between him and the road about equally. There was so much she wanted to say. So much that needed asking. She had found him. He was in her car. They had never had a funeral. Maureen wouldn't hear of it, and Dana had never been up to it anyway. He had died without ceremony, just been declared dead. What, exactly, had stopped her from taking seriously any of the short-lived boyfriends she'd briefly had in the years since?

Did he look like Franklin? How much did they resemble each other? Would Franklin see a resemblance? Would he guess who Reynolds was? He was a smart boy, smarter than Dana. What should she say? She almost asked that question aloud, but checked herself; the answer was up to her alone. Was her staring making him uncomfortable? For his part, he didn't look her way once. He was looking at the street, where he had lived, for how long? Why was he living that way, panhandling? What did he think about how she looked? What had the nearly ten years done to her? Did he recognize her? Did he smoke cigarettes in her backyard?

As she turned the car into the lot, she saw two people talking outside the store. One she instantly recognized as her son even from the distance. The other looked to be an adult, a man, who hovered closely over Franklin. The man, wearing a beige jacket and khaki pants, looked up, reacting to something Franklin had said. He turned and walked away quickly as Dana pulled up.

Dana didn't know how to introduce them. At no time did she contemplate telling the truth. That would be something for another day, after all the questions had been asked and answered, after she knew what Warren Reynolds had become.

"You're late," Franklin said. He was going to say more, but saw Reynolds and asked her who's this and why does he look like that, all with one facial expression.

"Climb in back," Dana said. Franklin was already opening the back door.

She glanced at Reynolds, who nodded to Franklin and then turned back in his seat to face the front.

Franklin had a plastic bag with a stack of comics in it.

Dana asked him who he'd been talking to.

Franklin pulled out his comics. "I've already read them all, waiting for you."

"Answer my question. Who was that man?"

"He walks fast."

"What?" Dana turned to Reynolds.

He shrugged. "He walks fast."

Franklin said, "He's just some guy who offered me a ride when I'd been out there for an hour."

"You didn't say you'd go with him, did you?"

"I'd like credit for having some brains, thank you."

"Never ride with a stranger."

"Never heard that before. They should tell you that in kindergarten."

"Franklin—"

"Sorry."

Dana turned about in her seat and faced him squarely. "No, I was going to say I'm sorry I was so late. No good excuse."

He shrugged. But his face said, *okay.*

"Did the man say who he was? Had you seen him before? Creep."

"He was in the store for a while. Didn't know anything about comics though."

"And not that it's going to happen again," Dana said, "but wait inside next time." Then she took a breath. "Franklin, this is an old friend, William. We haven't seen each other in a while."

Reynolds looked at her, but did not give her away.

"Hello, Franklin."

"Hi."

Dana eyed Reynolds. She had expected more curiosity from him. Was he wondering about Franklin's age? Did he realize this was his son?

"Mom, let's get going."

"Okay. Sorry."

XI. PLEASE DON'T LEAVE ME

She told Nessie a partial truth, which some might call a lie of omission. She said more to a co-worker she hardly knew two days before that co-worker retired. Years later, she told Brenda that she and Reynolds hadn't been getting along at the time of the accident. That was the best she could do, the closest she could get to vocalizing why Reynolds was dead.

The car hydroplaned. It turned sideways. It was airborne. Only the tires and the rear third of the car made contact with the guardrail. She was told that later.

She screamed. She recalls her scream vividly, how it whirled about her in the cabin of the car just as the car itself spun. Her head hit the passenger-side window. She screamed, "Reynolds." Reynolds grunted, trying to say something. There was blackness and the car flew into it. And it all happened quicker than you could tell it.

They were at a party given by an assistant principal. Reynolds had not wanted to go and that's what Dana later told Nessie they had been arguing about when Reynolds stomped on the gas as they tore through the downpour.

After discovering that telltale milk carton on the kitchen table, Dana had endured three days of waiting for the hammer to fall, torturous days wondering what he knew and when was he going to bring it up. He was acting differently, more reserved. He pecked her on her cheek when he came home and he did not ask her about her day; he simply retreated to the den and the television and when she was brave enough to look in on him, she saw a man bathed in the TV light like a statue, unseeing.

She instructed Steve not to be at the party. It was practically all she said to him in the days after their being caught; she left him to wonder what was going on and figure things out for himself.

She thought of what she would say to Reynolds when his cool, dark seething finally erupted. In those first couple of days, she wanted only to extricate herself from the mess. When confronted, she planned to say she had felt their relationship drifting a bit, losing its passion, and that she had simply reached out to a friend and then gotten in over her head. It made it sound like the affair wasn't entirely her fault, and that it had not been quite intentional, but rather just happenstance. But the longer he waited to say anything, the more her excuse seemed to fray at the edges. What drifting? Where? She had never mentioned any sense of drift. Reynolds and Dana had still been intimate all during the affair. They had made vacation plans. They had still eaten together and laughed together. But there must have been drifting—otherwise, why had she done it?

At the party, the night of the accident, three different friends came up to her at different points in the evening and asked her what was wrong. Each time she had forced a smile and replied that it was nothing. Reynolds took refuge in a circle of men, not speaking, but feigning interest in the talk. When she could take his sullenness no longer—or rather when she could no longer stomach her own anxiety—she decided to get it out in the open.

It had occurred to her that he might hit her. Never before had he laid hands upon her in anger, but they had never had a real argument before, just flare-ups. She was not afraid of getting hit.

She walked from one side of Mr. Lurie's living room to the other, around the small circles of people. She kept her eyes on Reynolds, who saw her coming, but refocused on whoever was talking in his group.

She put a hand on her husband's arm. She whispered, "Let's go. You were right, bad idea."

"You sure?"

In response she pulled on his arm. He made quick excuses to the teachers he'd been listening to as she steered him away.

She had not realized how hot it had been at the party until they stepped outside. It was drizzling already then, but still she could see a little bit of the moon, so she thought the rain probably wouldn't amount to much. Reynolds said just about the same thing. He opened the car door for her. She loved Reynolds very much. *I want to keep him*, she said to herself.

"So why'd you want to leave early?" He started the car. The street was clogged with parked cars. He looked about.

"Suddenly didn't feel into it."

"Huh." After a moment, when they were well on their way, she asked, "Do they still look at you funny?"

"What? What for?"

"You know, the only mixed couple on faculty or staff."

"Oh, no. Not really."

He pulled onto the interstate past the lit strip malls, south where it became narrower and overhung by trees. The rain began to fall with determination.

Dana felt the butterflies in her stomach. She dared not wait until they were home. Her courage would falter. Now, she would have to talk while they were in close proximity, while the only noise was rain splatter, while it was just them. She was going to bring it up now. She had her explanation ready. She would plead for him not to leave. *Say it*, she told herself.

Reynolds had to set the wipers to continuous.

She found herself mute. It may have been the first time in her life she was truly frightened.

Miles whipped by.

He had not turned on the radio, though usually he did so automatically. Did he sense something, had he been waiting for her to bring it up?

She opened her mouth. She looked at his dark profile, delineated by dashboard light. "Please, Reynolds. Please don't leave me," she said.

He looked at her, as they hurtled for what must have been a hundred yards through the black rain, before returning his gaze to the road. He slapped the steering wheel. "Don't, huh?"

"I love you, Reynolds. I'm still in love with you. I…I'm just a little stupid, too. It was stupid."

"That's not stupid, honey. It's betrayal, it's disrespectful, it's cruel—"

"I'm sorry—"

"Fuck sorry! Who was he? Was it that PE teacher?"

"Why do…yes. Steve."

"I must look like a fool to the entire faculty. That's why you dragged me to that damn lame party tonight? To show off the fool?"

"They don't know. No one does. No one knows but you."

"Damn. Damn and damn."

She'd forgotten her explanation, something about drifting apart. Tears were rolling down his face.

Neither of them realized how fast he must have been going. He passed other cars.

He said, "In my bed."

"I know. I'm sorry."

She was going to wipe his tears away. She thought the gesture would show she cared. She reached for his face and he batted her hand away.

The car fishtailed.

"Reynolds!"

Then he shoved her. Pushed her to the far side of the car.

"Why?" he said. "Why. Why. Why!"

The car spun and lifted. She hit her head on the passenger-side glass. She screamed. She was aware they were off the road. She shouted her husband's name. The car was heading downward and she couldn't account for that. The windshield cracked from a collision with a low-hanging limb from a tree they narrowly missed. Her head hit the passenger-side column and glass again, this time shattering it. Then came the splash, though Dana wasn't sure if she remembered hearing it or supplied that detail later.

All movement stopped.

She could not say how long she had been unconscious, but she had the feeling that it had been a long while. Rain beat on the roof. She felt nauseous and thick headed. She opened her eyes slowly, expecting to find that the car had spun out on the shoulder of the road. Many of her memories of the accident would not surface for several days. When she did not see the traffic and the road and its regularly placed overhead lamps, she realized she was disoriented. The utter blackness around her started the panic, which is also when the pain started. As soon as she moved, the pain ignited and she gasped. It was too late to be still now; the pain branched through her like a living, hungry thing. She cried. She took shallow breaths. She felt her face and head and her hand came away slick with blood. "Reynolds," she whispered. She wanted him to be okay and she wanted help. No answer came. She slowly turned her head toward the driver's side. It was empty and the door was wide open.

"Reynolds!" she shouted.

It was impossible to see through the hard rain, cracked glass, and darkness. She could not see the front end of the car. Black water rippled over it. It was submerged, but she could not figure that out. Her feet were wet past her ankles and she assumed that was more blood.

She had not brought her phone. Reynolds's phone had been on the center console. Her hand cast about. Everything hurt.

She tried to unbuckle herself, but the pain lit up and she froze as if trying to hide. That's when she first felt the car wriggle, and the sensation was terrifying. She couldn't account for it, but someone was pushing at the car. The rain must have slowed because finally she heard the river and knew that was why the car was rocking.

Reynolds, where are you? In her subsequent recurring dreams, this is when Reynolds knocks on her window with his bloody hand, smiling behind the web of cracked glass. He smiles at her and runs away. Sometimes he swims away.

She heard the knock. It startled her and she suspected she had again been unconscious. Pieces of glass fell in her lap. Cold water lapped about her legs. "Reynolds?" It was a fireman in black and yellow. He had appeared from out of the dark, an apparition just behind the shattered glass. She wasn't sure he was real. There was light now from somewhere and she saw the expanse of the river about her.

The fireman said, "We'll have you out of there in a moment, ma'am."

She said, "My husband. Find my husband."

"Driver's out," he said to someone behind him.

One man became a dozen. And then more.

They put a tarp over her face, then broke out the rest of the passenger-side glass.

"Ma'am, did your husband go for help?"

The nausea grew stronger. She tasted vomit. "What—"

Red and blue lights flitted about.

Maybe he had gone for help while she was unconscious. Climbed the embankment, tried to attract cars on the road.

It was a long time before they could remove her from the car.

"We'll get you out of this mess soon, ma'am."

"Did you find him?"

They took her vitals. They asked her name. They told her they'd had a lot of calls on account of the rain. They put a collar on her. Finally they brought a board from the driver's side. They had a hard time getting her on it, it seemed.

The river was everywhere.

"My feet are cold," she told them. "They're numb."

Half the car was submerged. Water was in the foot wells on both sides.

She could hear the water slapping the car, and the men, and the baritone idling of fire trucks from up the embankment.

Searchlights arced along the water, not penetrating. She gasped. Reynolds! "Oh, no. Oh, no."

The black water stretched out level around her, so close. The giant shapes of the highway bridge towers loomed as shadows. Frothy water jumped around the pilings.

They strapped her to the board.

"Here we go," they said.

The men massed about her to keep her level for the journey up. She could see their faces, hats, and the roiling clouds above them. There must have been at least six men carrying her. They called for each other to watch his step as they struggled with her up the embankment.

XII. DREAM TOO LOVELY

She had a thousand questions. She felt breathless. He entered her home and she said, "Have a seat." He sat at the kitchen table. He didn't look about and seemed to have no reaction to the few items that may have been familiar to him. She asked if he was hungry and he said he could eat, and Franklin said, "Me too."

"Have you got all your homework done for Monday?"

"All done."

"Then go read your comics."

"I read them. Remember, the hour wait?"

He seemed determined not to leave his mother alone with this man he did not know. After forgetting him for more than an hour, she had lost her moral authority for the evening.

"Let's see," Dana said. The man and the boy sat at the kitchen table.

Franklin slid his comics out of the bag.

"I can make you hotdogs," she said to her son. "And what about a salad?" she asked Reynolds.

"I'd like a hotdog too, if you have it."

"Oh, sure."

"Comics," he said to Franklin.

"Yeah."

Dana had to resist the temptation to stare at him. She tried to put more focus on broiling hotdogs and defrosting buns than required. But with each move and turn her eyes returned to the man at her kitchen table. *Just breathe*, she thought, *for now*.

"I have a complete run of Thor. Since *Journey into Mystery* number 83."

"Yeah?"

"Yeah. My dad left them to me, mostly. But I've kept the run going."

Dana froze.

"Thor's cool."

"You know about Thor?"

"I think they should have kept him with Jane Foster. I mean, Sif is more his speed, being a warrior and a goddess and all, but I liked the whole immortal-with-a-human dynamic."

Franklin grinned. He looked to Dana, who thought she smiled back at him.

Despite everything, what she really struggled to hold back was a rampant giddiness.

It didn't make sense and she knew it. What she should have done was slap him across his face in the Serve parking lot and drive away. Just let him know she knew what kind of fraud he really was. Who would let all your loved ones, wife, mother, sister, friends, believe you dead? Yet she had hugged him. He didn't smell all that good. But if Franklin were not there, she would hug him again.

"Mustard and relish?"

The year Reynolds disappeared, life and death had vied for her. These forces sent her into depression over the past and apprehension for the future. Her body was changing as drastically as her life had changed. Through all of it, she never forgot she only had herself to blame. Unable to sleep on her back or stomach, she propped herself on pillows and kept the television running all night. She had screwed up her past and now could not escape it, because she carried it right in front of her.

Maureen kept telling her Reynolds was alive. Ness stayed out of it for the most part. Dana suspected both were ready to sever all ties with her—until they learned she was pregnant.

She made them two hotdogs each and placed a slice of pickle on each plate. "We usually eat better," she said.

"No, we don't."

She asked him if he wanted milk or juice. They both asked for milk. She watched them eat. Reynolds inspected the covers of Franklin's comics, being careful not to drip mustard on them. He was too calm.

Franklin was eating up the man's interest.

What he had done to her was much worse than what she had done to him.

He left behind the clock he gave her for her birthday. And the place where he threw his sneakers when he came in from mowing. He left the showerhead he had installed. He left the loveseat they had sex on that was so good they tried it three more times afterward, but never quite recaptured that same erotic heat. He left his coffee cup with the Redskins logo on it. His towel; he liked the green one, and so she would use it sometimes just to get a rise out of him. One time she wrapped herself in it and he said, "Hey, that's my towel," and spun her out of it and into his arms. She saw these things everywhere—stuffed animals he'd gotten her, presents she'd gotten him. He was everywhere, reminding her, accusing her. This is what he had done to her.

He asked for more milk.

One evening, she brought home a box from school, a big one that textbooks had been delivered in. When she made up her mind to do it, to clear the field of all those mines, she darted about the house with more speed than she had mustered in a long time. His comb and cologne she dropped into the box without sniffing the bottle. His trimmer from his sink. That green towel. His magazines, his shoes, the watch she gave him—all went into the box, banging against whatever she had already dropped in as she rooted about for more. She sprinted from dresser to nightstand, room to room, purging the house of all that would fit in the box. She took a framed Jacob Lawrence poster off the wall, a black couple sitting on a green couch. It was too big for the box so she sat it at the front door. She filled the box to the top. Her tummy began to hurt from all the activity.

She sat heavily on her bed, which used to be their bed but wouldn't fit in the box. She told Franklin, who she didn't know at the time was Franklin, to quit complaining. She grabbed the stuffed dog. Spot the Fun Dog, they'd named it. It looked at her with big black eyes and an eternal smile. She flipped it into the box. It tumbled and landed upright, staring back at her. She would need ten boxes to complete this exorcism. She would need to box the house. She drew her legs up and lay on her side, curling herself around her tummy. *Mommy is sorry she ran you around like that.* The baby responded, moved a bit, and then settled, and the pain went away. *Well, thank you, sweetie.* The baby became a blessing to her, her child unseen, a blessing no matter what—no matter his paternity—and she talked to him every night thereafter at length, long conversations sometimes that wound here and there, stories of Reynolds, stories of her, stories that got her through the darkest moments.

"Franklin, go on upstairs so the adults can talk."

"How come? I want to stay." The look on Dana's face must have quelled his rebellion. "Fine," he said. He shoved his chair away with the backs of his legs.

"Take your comics."

"I am."

"Franklin, it's cool you kept your dad's run going there."

"Yeah."

"For a few minutes, sweetie."

"Whatever."

He made as much noise as he could as he left. The adults watched him go.

"He's a real good boy, actually."

"I can tell that."

"Good."

She sat down opposite him.

One side of his face looked as if it had been rouged with dirt. Shoots of kinky hair made him look like a wild man.

"Warren," she said.

"You said my name was William."

She pointed toward the stairs. "I told *him* your name was William."

He had an amused expression and pretended as if he were trying to contain it.

Instantly, Dana wanted to remove it.

"I don't see anything funny," she said. She was going to say something about his mother, about her illness, but she held back.

"I guess it isn't. Why did you tell your son my name is William? I'm confused."

"I don't think he's ready to hear the truth yet." She lowered her voice, remembering how words carried in the little town house. "Any more than you seem ready to tell it."

He scratched at the back of his head. He smelled—not as bad as Jessie, but more than bad enough. *Maybe this wasn't the right time*, Dana thought. He was here. Her husband was sitting at her kitchen table. Maybe that had to be enough for the moment. A hint of the smirk returned. He scratched the side of his face; it sounded as if he were scratching sandpaper.

"Do you want to take a shower? And I have your old clothes. Think they still fit?"

"You kept them, huh?"

"I didn't throw away anything."

"How long has it been? Time just winds away from me. Days blur, weeks blur…"

"Nine years and four months."

He looked at her then and the smirk was gone. His eyes took her in and, for the first time, Dana saw something warm and soft and sympathetic in them. "Dana, that's a long, damn time," he said quietly.

His rough hand took one of hers, not completely; he simply caught two of her fingers and rubbed them gently with his thumb.

The touch sent a pulse through her. Her eyes welled. She felt she would break down completely if she didn't move away. She gave his hand a gentle squeeze before pulling hers back. She wiped her eyes. "That shower, how about it?" She stood. She tasted saltiness as the corners of her mouth. "And I can find those clothes in the meantime."

He nodded, but made no move to rise. "How long have you been looking for me?"

"For months after you disappeared, but the baby came and I... but then every day since I spotted you."

"Spotted me? Where?"

"You were—you were at 28 and Liberia Avenue."

"Oh."

"C'mon." She motioned and left the kitchen. She heard him following.

With the shower running, she wrestled boxes in the guest bedroom closet.

Franklin came in. He startled her and she jumped.

"He's taking a shower?"

"Yes. Is that okay with you?"

He shrugged. "Strange."

"Not strange. Look, he's an old acquaintance, a friend, who's down on his luck, okay? We'll just help him a little bit, okay?"

She found the clothes. She found Spot the Fun Dog. She picked out a pair of brown pants and a white pullover. She found socks and a pair of tan shoes and underclothes. She carried these to the bathroom and hesitated at the door. She wanted to see him. Dana knocked and entered.

"Don't freak. Just leaving the clothes."

A dark shape turned behind the translucent glass. "What?"

"The clothes."

"Thank you, Dana."

"You're welcome," she shouted above the water spray. "More than welcome," she said quietly while closing the door.

In her bedroom, Dana looked at herself in her vanity mirror. She took up a brush and started punishing her hair. Her looks weren't what they were ten years ago. There was skin at her elbows. Her jawline was less distinct. She'd kept her figure for the most part, but everything was saggier. *That's a long, damn time.*

He reappeared downstairs. The hair on his head and face was temporarily subdued by dampness. He wore the shirt and pants. The pants were baggy. And he wore his beat-up sneakers instead of the tan shoes. He had his coat under his arm and he seemed embarrassed by it now.

"Shoes didn't fit. A little tight."

"People's feet spread when they get older. Sometimes they have to go up a size."

"I hadn't heard that." The smirk returned briefly. "I feel like a new man," he said.

Dana felt the nervousness in her grow. "Any woman will tell you, new shoes are good for renewal too. We'll go buy you a pair." She flashed on Jessie and her green shoes.

"Oh, well, thank you, but these still have a lot of life left in them."

"It wouldn't be a problem."

He didn't reply.

They stood a couch-length apart. The awkwardness stretched out. She was surprised by her inability to start, to say all the things she wanted to say and ask. "Sit. Please. Have a seat."

"I'd best be going."

Her nervousness was identified right then. If she moved too quickly, she sensed he would be lost to her again. This reunion did not mean the same to him as it meant to her, not yet at least. She feared he would run. "We haven't caught each other up yet."

"Well…"

She sat down, but he didn't follow her cue.

"Dana, I better leave you and your boy be. I have to get going."

"No. I mean, why?"

"I have a job in the morning. I'm helping a man put up a shed. Me and another guy."

"You're helping…" She stood. *Don't want to miss that golden opportunity*, Dana thought. "You can stay here and I'll drive you over there in the morning. I mean, you can't just go. You…"

"We can meet up again, after the job."

"Where's the job?"

"Not sure. The man drives; I don't pay attention."

"Where will we meet? At Serve?"

"Downtown is closer to you. He drives through downtown at the end of the day. We'll meet at the train station, at six. All right?" He smiled.

"You don't have a place to stay."

"I do. Got a roof for now, me and some others. Will you give me a ride?"

She nodded. "I wish you…" And then she said without thinking, "Are you happy to see me?"

He looked at her for a long moment.

Dana saw him through blurred vision. She lowered her head. *Stupid question.*

He let his coat that he'd been carrying under an arm slip to the floor and he closed the short distance between them. He hugged her to him. Her face was on his chest. He smelled of soap this time. Dana put her arms around him. "Dana," he said. "You are a dream too lovely to believe in."

Franklin came down just as they were going through the door. Reynolds told him he would see him tomorrow. He told him he wanted to see his comic collection.

"Cool," Franklin said.

She drove him to Old Town Manassas. Before he got out of her car, Reynolds asked if she had any change she could spare. "He's going to pay us tomorrow…for helping him build the shed. I can get it back to you then."

Dana dug through her wallet. She had twenty-three dollars in fives and ones. She gave it all to him. "Tomorrow," she said.

Tomorrow came. Six p.m. finally came. She had thought she would be useless at work, anticipating seeing him again, but she had done well, engaged the children and laughed with them. They had taken her mind off the situation. After microwaving dinner for Franklin, she had hurried over to the train station. She watched the commuters unload from the VRE. They moved with purpose to their cars.

She expected to see a pickup truck come rattling up. He would jump out the back of it. The fresh clothes she had given him yesterday would be soiled and sweaty from the day's toil. No matter; another shower, more clothes; she would feed him something, send Franklin to his room or to Brenda's, and Reynolds and she could talk, on the couch or at the kitchen table. There was so much to talk about. So much to say that she wasn't sure what needed to be said anymore, or what needed to be let go. Maybe she could tell him about his mother.

Ness had called when Dana got home from work. Maureen wasn't doing well. The chemo was "beating her down" and she wanted to see Franklin again.

Ness had that defensive edge in her voice. Ready to cut Dana off if she said the wrong thing.

"I'll bring him down as soon as I can. Saturday at the latest."

"You will?" Ness said. "I don't have to come up there and yank your hair or anything?"

The humor in Ness's voice surprised Dana. "No violence necessary."

"'Cause I will, you know." And then her sister-in-law, who Dana realized was actually still her sister-in-law, said, "Thanks, Dana."

She didn't tell Ness about Reynolds. It was still her secret for a while, too nascent, too fragile to share.

She was sitting on a bench near the ticket machine. She was inside her own thoughts, and only pulled back to the here-and-now when the giant train filled her view and the lines of passengers streamed from it.

Hours later, the last commuter train had long since left. A long freight train roared and jangled by. The sun had set. Dana checked her watch and feared she had lost him again. Second chances are so rare as to be almost impossible. A couple or three hours one afternoon had been her second chance and she had blown it. *Are you happy to see me?* That was not the question she had wanted to ask. She walked around the building a few times. Maybe he had been waiting on the other side, any other side.

Her car was parked far away. When she had arrived, the commuters' cars filled the station lots and all the side streets for blocks. Across the tracks was a little restaurant and she could see families and couples eating in there under soft lights. Not wanting to give up her wait, she watched them for a while, saw the waitress talking to them, saw them eat, saw animated conversation, and could even hear laughter now and then.

She had to think a moment before she recalled where she had parked her car.

XIII. EVEN CHIP WOULDN'T HELP

At the diner, Reynolds sulks the entire time. He's trying to punish her, Dana speculates, for not being what he wants her to be. He wants her miserable, like him. She thinks marriage ought to be more lighthearted than this, not so wearing and wearying.

Earlier that evening, Dana had returned home from a long day at school tired from the feet up. She walked through their empty apartment, through the kitchen, and back to the front room and dropped onto the couch. She kicked off her shoes and discovered with delight that the remote was actually within reach. She clicked on the TV and then brought one foot to her lap and began to rub her instep with her thumb.

She watched the news without consuming one piece of information. She had fallen asleep, or nearly so, when she looked up to see Reynolds standing across the room looking at her.

He was loosening his tie.

"Hey," she said.

"Hey," he returned, and in that one syllable she could sense his shortness and frustration.

"What, honey?"

"Would it have been so hard for you to have some dinner on? I mean, at least get something started? Damn."

"I wor—"

"I work too." He waved a dismissive hand at her.

"Don't do that," she said, coming to her feet. The remote fell from her lap to the carpet. "Don't do that to me." She was next to him instantly, staring into his face. "Don't wave me off like that."

He looked at her, not angrily, but appraisingly. He turned to walk away, shaking his head.

"Hey, Reynolds," she said.

He breathed out loudly and said he'd had a long, hard day. "They gave the assignment I wanted to someone else."

"That's shitty."

His chin moved, a nearly imperceptible nod.

"You gave them the idea to go for that account in the first place."

"Well, my team did."

"Still...shitty."

"Still," he said, "and watch your language." There was a small smile.

She took the opening and suggested they go out to dinner. Besides, there wasn't a clean dish in the kitchen.

"I just want to crash on the couch," he said.

"No, come on. Drop your tie on the floor. We'll go get a bite. You'll feel better; so will I. I'll commiserate."

It is a bad idea.

Reynolds works himself into a real funk. He only plays with his food and hardly pays any attention to Dana. Dana gradually senses that some of his frustration is directed at her, but she shakes that notion away. She's done nothing but try to cheer him up and has been unrewarded. "Well, don't let it get you down," she says after a long silence.

He just looks at her.

She might say to him right now that she gets that he's angry and disappointed, but when she says things like that, it's as if he chooses not to believe her. And if she says nothing, she comes off as unfeeling. She thinks, not for the first time in this marriage, how different any two people are, and how foolish people are if they think they ever truly know another person. Even the simplest words seem to have different meanings and a touch can be interpreted two different ways. Their arguments hurt too much to do them any good, so they clip them off and rely on looks and shakes of the head. She gazes out the diner window at the dark parking lot. Constant judging, constant defending. *This is exhausting*, she thinks. *My feet hurt.*

Finally, the check is paid and they leave.

———————

They walk to the car. She places a hand on his upper arm, but he is walking quickly and doesn't seem to be aware that her hand is there.

She does not see the man at first. He was either already in the parking lot between two cars or came from behind them. He says something that Dana catches only fragments of "…keep…kind."

Reynolds explodes. Her hold on him is gone in an instant. Her husband is shoving a man who is taller than he is. The other man pushes back.

"Reynolds!"

Reynolds says to the man, "Why don't you keep out of my way and mind your own business?"

They are shoving and swinging. She sees her husband struck. They stagger awkwardly like two drunks dancing and fall against a truck. Reynolds almost falls and the tall man is upon him then and wraps an arm around her husband's neck.

"Stop it! Stop it!" She is shouting and casts about for help.

The man has Reynolds in a choke hold. Reynolds is doubled over gasping. His face is framed by the man's arm. Reynolds digs into that arm with his fingers.

Dana sees a couple several cars down and hails them with a waving arm. "Please!" she says.

They freeze. They seem to hold in place for an interminably long time. The man finally comes forward, the woman anchoring behind with a hand on his arm.

"Please, help my husband!"

"Lady, he looks like he's handling himself just fine."

"That man is choking my husband."

"Oh."

"No, Chip, come on," the wife says. "Come on." She is pulling him by the arm and after a moment, Chip lets her lead him away.

Dana shouts at the struggling men again.

Reynolds grunts loudly and lifts the man, who still has an arm around his neck. He slams the man against the cabin of a pickup truck. The car alarm is set off. The hold is broken and Reynolds shoves the man away. Dana thinks she should get between them, but does not move.

"Reynolds, let's go. Okay? Okay?"

The men snarl words at each other, but neither seems ready to resume the fight.

"Let's go, damn it!"

In the car, Dana reaches across Reynolds to lock his door and then lock hers.

"Damn it," she says again. Her heart races but she feels relief too.

Reynolds's hand is trembling. He starts the car. His lips are tight. The snarl is still on his face. "Fucking bastard," he says.

Reynolds drives out of the lot, craning about for another glimpse of the man, but they don't see him.

"What the hell happened? Did he hit you? I mean before. Did he bump you or something?"

Reynolds had a hard grip on the steering wheel.

"Hon?"

They are waiting at a light. Red coats his face. "Didn't you hear what he said?"

"Just a word or two. No."

"He said, 'Why don't you keep to your own kind?'"

"Redneck-ass jerk."

"Where were you?"

"What?"

They are driving again.

"If Ness were there she'd have been all over that bastard. She would have scratched his eyes out or something. *Most* women I know would have weighed in while their man was in a goddamn headlock."

This is stunning. "You wanted me to join the fight?"

"I'm just saying."

"Well, you can shut up now."

The rest of the drive is silent. Entering the house is silent. Watching TV in separate rooms is silent. Getting ready for bed is silent. In the bed, Dana cries. She thinks she is doing that silently too. Her face lies on a soaked pillowcase.

She hears Reynolds's voice ask, "Well, Miss, why are you crying?"

She wants him to leave her in peace for the rest of the night. She sniffs. "I was on my feet all day. My feet hurt."

The mattress rocks her as Reynolds moves. The spread and sheet are pulled back and he gathers her feet onto his lap. He begins a massage, rubbing his thumbs into them, working the pads and the toes, caressing the instep. It feels very, very good.

When he is done, he kisses her toes, which tickles, and slips her feet back under the sheets.

"I wasn't just standing idly by watching," she says. "I was scoring the fight. Adding points for escaping the headlock, you won four to two."

"Yeah?"

"Yep."

"Huh." He curls around her. A protective arm drapes over her. "Strangely, that makes me feel better."

XIV. LUCKY YOU

Dana was crossing the train platform when she heard something behind her, a scraping sound.

"Hey."

A man was behind her, and not far. She almost said Reynolds's name, but this wasn't him. This man had a funny lean, a bent way he held himself. He held his arms up in front. *Like a goat on two legs*, Dana thought. He looked like bones and rags.

She looked about. The nearest people were in the restaurant, across a lot and three train tracks.

"Hey," he said again.

"I'm sorry, I don't have any change," she said. She had given all her cash to Reynolds yesterday. Then it occurred to her that maybe Reynolds had sent this goat man, maybe he had a message for her.

"Do you know Warren Reynolds?"

"No. Do you?"

"What? I—" She started walking.

She could feel him following after her.

"Hey."

She turned. "Fuck off!" She picked up her pace.

He still followed as she left the platform and headed down the street.

Her car was three blocks away. As she walked, she fished out her cell phone and made sure it was on. She should have headed for the restaurant, but she had thought only about gaining the safety of her car first.

"Hey."

They passed the darkened doors and windows of closed businesses. She was going to turn around and shout *leave me alone*, but she had already told him to fuck off to no avail and didn't want to slow down for a second. She covered another block at nearly a run. She was in the old residential section now. Old, giant trees canopied everything in shadow. Her breathing was loud. Her shoes

111

clacked loudly on the pavement. When she got to the corner, she turned to check how far behind the goat man was.

Dana squealed.

He was in arm's reach directly behind her. He had been running with her the entire time.

"Hey, you tell me to fuck off, huh."

Dana thumbed the nine and a one on her cell.

Goat Man grabbed her hand, squeezing it tightly over the phone. "What are you doing?"

"Let go of me, God damn it. Leave me alone."

"You leave me alone."

She wrenched her hand free, but her phone sailed away from her. She did not see where it went, but she heard it hit the ground.

Dana put a hand out, palm toward him, fingers spread. "Stop. Stop!"

"You stop. You stop."

"Me?"

"You always disturbin' around my spot. My spot."

"What?" Dana thought she recognized him.

The man's arms flailed out. His chest heaved outward. He staggered toward Dana. He squeaked.

Someone had come up from behind him. This second man punched Goat Man on the side of his face and then in his ribs. Goat Man's hands went up defensively.

The man pushed Goat Man, then punched him in the face. Dana heard the sickening thump.

Goat Man wobbled backwards, holding his face. "Oh. Oh."

Dana said, "Wait." She looked around for her cell phone.

The second man punched Goat Man again, who cried out a non-sensible string of words.

"Get," the second man said. "Then get." He made as if he were going to throw another punch, drawing his arm back deliberately.

Goat Man, looking more than ever as if balanced on hind legs, held his hands to his face, and spit a string of drool and unintelligible words. He staggered across the street, moving in one direction and then another. He fell between two cars.

Dana searched for her phone.

"Are you all right?" the man asked her.

"We've got to call about that man."

"To have him arrested?"

Dana's phone rang. It was under the nearest car. She lowered herself to her knees.

"Let me get that."

"No, I've got it. We should call an ambulance."

"For him? He's okay. Look."

"Hello," Dana answered her phone.

Still cursing, Goat Man was on his feet, moving away, bent at an angle.

"Bastard's fine." He put a hand out to help her up.

Dana brushed her hair back. She accepted the offered hand.

"Mom, when are you coming home? Did you find William?"

There was something wet on his hand. She took hers away as quickly as politeness let her.

"Hi, baby."

"Did you find William?"

"No. I didn't." She turned away from the man and said, "Call me back in ten minutes. Ten. If you don't hear from me call—call Brenda. I'm on Chauncey and Third Street." She broke the connection before Franklin could ask all his questions. There was blood on her hands. She rubbed at it with the ball of her thumb.

"I've always wanted to do that."

"Beat someone?"

"No. Rescue a damsel in distress."

"Thank you…"

"Doug, Doug Peel." He held out the same hand.

"Thank you, Doug. Dana. There's something on your hand."

He inspected both his hands.

"Is that his or yours?"

He didn't reply. Apparently, he didn't have a handkerchief. Dana had no tissues in her purse and apologized. He worked his hands together, rubbing them furiously. "Think it's his, though my knuckles are really hurting. I think they're swelling."

"You should get that looked at."

"Hazards of being a knight."

He walked closer to the nearest street lamp. He inspected his hands. Dana followed him.

"I guess he'll look over his shoulder before he accosts another woman."

"I don't know what he wanted."

Doug Peel looked up from his hands. "He grabbed you, didn't he?" he said defensively.

"Oh, yes, yes. He terrified me. Chased me down the street."

"I saw. And you didn't know this one?"

"I was just thinking...no. No idea who he was." Dana was thinking that maybe she did know Goat Man. He may have been the homeless man who lived in the bushes on the side of the museum, who she had shown Reynolds's picture to on two or three occasions. She had invaded his bush and cardboard box home more than once. Disturbing his sleep. Trespassing.

"Can I walk you to your car, or do you live around here?"

He was her height. He had black hair, which was combed straight back, and a prominent chin that pushed out from his face farther than his lips did. Dana had seen him someplace before.

She was conscious of Doug Peel standing near her, closer than she would like. A man on his porch, backlit by light from his opened doorway, called to them. Dana could not see his face. "Is everyone all right out there?" He sounded elderly. "Do I need to call the police?"

"No," Doug said.

"No, thank you. We're fine. Thanks."

He hesitated going back inside. Dana and Doug watched him. In high school, a boy once grabbed her by her wrist and pulled her into a coat closet. He put his hands on her. She managed to kick the door open and screamed so loudly that teachers and students converged from everywhere. The boy claimed he was joking and that Dana had overreacted. Dana recalled that his look of perplexed innocence was very convincing.

The man went back inside.

Doug looked at Dana. "A little late with the offer, don't you think?" He blew on his right hand. She wasn't sure what had her more rattled, Goat Man chasing her or Peel punishing him.

She recognized Peel now. He was the man who had offered her a ride the rainy night she had first spotted Reynolds. He had run up to her with a newspaper over his head.

"Damn." He shook his hands. "So, you walking home or to your car?"

"Car."

"I'll escort you."

She was about to decline, but Goat Man was out there somewhere nursing his bruises and maybe getting angrier. "This way." She pointed, smiled, and they began walking.

"Lucky you I was down this way. I was going to a restaurant—by myself, which I hate—but it was too crowded; I'd have had to wait forever. So I went for a walk instead. Hey, they're probably calling my table number now. You hungry?"

Dana chuckled. "You were very brave to come help."

When they went under another street lamp, Dana studied his face.

"I don't know. I saw the chase. And it took me a second to tell my feet what to do."

"I had a scare recently and I just froze."

"I think the freezing is instinct. You know, ancient cave man probably froze when a dinosaur or a saber tooth was hunting him. You know, to avoid detection."

"Ah, interesting theory."

"Are you teasing me?"

"Not at all. I'm sure there's something to it."

They walked in silence for a while. Dana said something about how different a neighborhood looks at night.

He inspected his hands.

They arrived at Dana's car just as her phone rang. "Hey, honey. All's well. No. I'll tell you all about it when I get home."

Dana opened her door and eased behind the wheel. She stuck her keys in the ignition. She went to shut the door, but Peel held on to it.

"Well—"

"So you didn't say what brought you out here."

"Oh, I was supposed to meet a friend, but I guess we got our plans crossed."

"Well, I hope you did meet a friend."

"Thank you. You and I met before."

"I was wondering if you remembered," he said. He smiled. "Your cart ran into mine at Shoppers Warehouse."

"Oh." Her mind began to whirl.

"I should have gotten your number then. There was hidden damage to that cart." He laughed.

Dana remembered the incident, but hadn't paid any attention to the man's face then. Her mind kept racing.

"Can I get your number now?"

"Um. You know, thank you for the rescue."

"Look, you turned me down for a bite to eat—"

"I thought you were joking."

"At least you can give me your number." His face tightened.

Dana wanted to pull the door closed. "I'll tell you what, gallant knight." She forced a big smile. "You give me your number like a gentlemanly knight, and this damsel will give you a call."

"Sure?" he asked.

"We'll go to that restaurant that you didn't want to go to alone."

"Have you got pen and paper?"

"I have my phone."

She keyed in "DP" and the number. He repeated the number. "Have it," Dana said.

He stepped from the door and Dana closed it, feeling the relief like a hug.

He was waving at her.

She returned the wave as she pulled her car from the curb.

In her rear view, she saw him still standing in the street. He was lighting a cigarette. The lighter made a glowing spot of his face.

XV. DANA AND MAUREEN

They went to visit Maureen. Leaving town brought a little bit of relief. The farther down the road they went, the better she breathed. Dana's head churned with so many fears she couldn't think straight. There was the fear a stalker had latched on to her. The fear that stalker knew where she lived. The fear for Franklin's safety. The fear she had lost Reynolds. The fear she had no control over whatever came next. And the fear she would have to keep living the life she had now.

When she arrived home after being rescued by Doug Peel, she was greeted at the door by Franklin, who had a stream of questions. She could tell he had been frightened by the phone conversation they'd had.

She never knew how much was appropriate to tell him anymore. He seemed mature in many ways, but still her little baby in others.

"First of all, everything is okay, right? Franklin, look at me. Everything is okay."

"Okay."

"Some flaky guy was following me to my car, but another man came along and chased him away. But I didn't like the looks of the second man, either, so I told you to stand by just in case."

"It was hard to wait ten minutes."

She hugged him. "Oh, honey, I bet it was."

"It took forever." He said into her shoulder.

"It took forever for me, too. C'mon, let's go over to Brenda's. I want to talk to her."

"I'm gonna stay here and watch TV."

"No. Let's go. Get your shoes on."

Franklin looked at his mother's face and for some reason did not argue.

"Hey, girl," Brenda greeted her at the door. Her smile drooped. "What's wrong?"

"What are they watching upstairs?" Franklin asked.

"I don't know, buddy. Go find out," she said without taking her eyes off Dana.

"I'm frazzled. Brenda, I think I picked me up a stalker."

"Shit."

"Is Geoff here? We need some male, testosterone, manhood..."

"Geoff will have to do. Geoff! Geoff! Living room."

She told her friends everything. She told them about having found Reynolds.

"It's him? Really? After all this time?"

"Omigod, Dana! And now he's stalking you?"

"No. Somebody else."

"Oh, Dana, honey...it can't really be your Reynolds."

"Don't do that. Don't talk to me that way, like I'm a moron."

"Did he say he was Warren Reynolds?"

Dana gave her friend a look, but inside tried to review her conversations with Reynolds. Her mind was too frenetic to recall anything.

"*Ladies.* Get back to the stalker first, Dana."

She told them what had just happened. She told them about the Goat Man and about her Doug Peel. "We've *accidentally* run into each other three times. Three times!"

"Well that's possible. Coincidences are unlikely things that happen anyway," Geoff said.

Dana said, "Oh...and he smokes."

"That cinches it."

"The cigarette butts in your backyard."

"Doug Peel."

"You didn't give him your last name, did you? Just in case he isn't the backyard prowler?"

"I wonder if that's even his real name?"

"No. I didn't. I have his phone number too."

Brenda said, "Heck, let's give his name and number to the cops and have them tell this guy to cease and desist."

Geoff made a face.

"What?"

"I don't think she has anything. 'Excuse me, officer, this man saved me from a mugging, arrest him.'"

"You don't think...two times is a coincidence. Three times is stalking. Hey, did you keep those cigarette butts?"

Dana shook her head.

"They had his DNA on them."

"Oh, shit."

"What."

"I just thought...Franklin! Franklin!"

"The show's at the good part."

"Come down here."

He appeared to have already gotten over his fright. Dana wasn't sure that was a good thing. "One second and you can run back up. Franklin, the man you were talking to in front of the comic book shop, did he have a pronounced chin?" Dana stuck her chin out. "You know, Jay Leno?"

"Yeah, I guess so."

"That's all. Go back to your show."

"Why?"

"Go. I'll talk to you about it later."

He threw his hands up and ran back up the stairs. She turned back to Geoff and Brenda, who looked troubled.

Geoff said, "We'll call the cops. Just tell them everything, and see what they say."

"Can Franklin and I stay here tonight?"

"The sofa folds out," Brenda said.

———————————

In the following days, Dana's head turned back and forth so much her neck began to hurt. She hoped to spot Reynolds and feared she would see Doug Peel. She looked over her shoulder and in bushes and in parked cars constantly when going from house to car and car to school. She was afraid to go to the grocery store, let alone to go out searching for her husband.

She drove Franklin to school even though it made her late for work. She spoke to Franklin's teacher and principal. He was to be watched constantly while outside and to stay on school grounds, behind fences if possible.

Imagining Doug Peel sitting out there smoking, she would look into her backyard and shiver. She explained to Franklin that stalkers were sick people, but still very dangerous. She told him he could go nowhere alone for the time being. She told him he'd have to be wary. She repeated it so that she feared she might make him paranoid. "I get it," he said. One day after Franklin saw his mother looking out the back kitchen window, he said to her, "I put tacks on the patio chairs. Anybody sits on them at night is gonna go, yeoow!" Mother and son had had a laugh over that.

She wasn't eating much. She wasn't being much of a teacher, either.

Dana berated herself for finally deciding to call the police. Her story was difficult to tell while still keeping Reynolds's name out of it. He was the reason she had been out at night. He was the reason she could run her cart into someone and not see them. Her search for him was the reason Goat Man had chased her down the street.

Brenda had come with her to the police station while Franklin stayed with Geoff and the kids.

Officer Metz had only one expression, dubious. If you told him your name and showed him your driver's license to back it up, he would still have the same dubious, flat look on his face, his head angled slightly away while his eyes stayed on you. Brenda hadn't agreed with Dana's assessment of the officer, but she had been told to wait in the lobby while Dana told her mostly true story.

"Manassas isn't a big town," he replied to her story of having run into Doug Peel four times, counting his talking to Franklin in front of the comic-book shop. "But maybe it's a bit hinky," Dana replied. Metz said he'd run the name, then picked up his clipboard and left the little interview room. Dana felt that omitting any mention of Reynolds made her story a little less credible. She felt she was protecting him by leaving him out of all this. She didn't want to give him a reason to disappear again, if he hadn't already left.

"He's had a couple of traffic violations, Mrs. Reynolds," Metz said entering the room. "Speeding, improper lane change. I'm with you, though, something's hinky about him. You don't have anything a judge could use to support a restraining order. Tell you what—why don't you use the buddy system next time you go on one of these long walks of yours. You're doing the right thing, watching your boy all the way into the school building when you drop him off. Keep your doors locked, car and house. Get some pepper spray for peace of mind. Have your phone handy and charged. These are good practices anyway, stalker or no. Then forget about him."

"Forget about him? Officer, you're forgetting about the cigarette butts. I saw someone in my backyard."

"Well, there's no evidence of him trying to break in. I mean this Doug Peel, or whoever this is, right?"

Dana nodded reluctantly, not liking where he was heading. The officer seemed determined not to find anything for the police to do.

"Don't chase him away by turning on the lights next time. Just call us. Let him sit there and enjoy his smoke. We'll pick the garbage up for you."

Dana waited to hear more. He had not asked about the cigarette butts, which she didn't have anyway, but he should have asked, she felt; Brenda's DNA idea sounded good to Dana.

"Do you have dead bolt locks? Yes? Use them."

"That's it?" Dana could actually taste the anger in her mouth. She had to swallow. "Officer..."

"Mrs. Reynolds, if you had told him to leave you the heck alone and he persisted in making contact, then I could drop by and try to scare him off, at least give him a reason to think twice. But you encouraged him."

"Encouraged…"

"You took his name and number, probably smiled at him…we men find that encouraging."

"That's it?" Brenda had asked Dana as the two of them left the station.

"Yeah. Make sure I use my dead bolts."

"So Frankie's tacks are all we have?"

––––––

On the way to Maureen's, Franklin asked, "Why is that guy following us around, you think?"

They moved slowly down Highway 1, which alternated between tree-lined curves and long stretches of strip malls and car dealerships.

The air was cool. They had the windows cracked.

"They have a reason in their own minds, but it wouldn't make sense to us."

"He didn't know anything about comics. He said some stuff about Batman and the Joker, but you could tell he was taking it from that old TV show. I wish we could trap him. I wish we had one of those clamps with teeth that hunters use to catch wolves." He made a trap with his hands and curled fingers. "Smack! And we'd have him."

"It's going to be okay, honey. Okay?"

Her son didn't reply. He put on the earphones to his MP3 player and was silent for the remainder of the trip.

Ness answered the door at Maureen's. She and Franklin hugged immediately and for a lot longer than usual. Dana skirted around them and waited.

Dana went to the foyer window and looked out on the quiet street. Brown leaves scuttled along the sidewalk. Would he have followed her down here? He would want to know where she was going.

"Dana." Something was missing from Ness's face. The woman looked worried. Maybe she was worried Dana would bring up Reynolds again, that Reynolds nonsense. Ness's brows said she no longer had confidence.

"Hi, Ness." Reynolds once told her that as a boy he used to say "Your High-Ness." It would really get under her skin.

"We've temporarily turned the dining room into a downstairs bedroom. Frankie, the doctors have given your grandma some really strong medicines and it's wearing her down a bit, okay? So she looks a bit tired, okay?"

Franklin nodded. Dana could see he was instantly frightened.

The dining-room table had been pushed to the side and was being used to hold blankets and a tray and bottles of pills. The chairs were crowded into a corner. A bed, nightstand, and lamp had been brought down. The impression of Maureen's head was still in the pillow of the unmade bed. She sat in the wingback brought in from the living room.

Dana nearly gasped, but stopped herself and shut her mouth. A horrible transformation had taken place. But as she thought back, Maureen was already being reduced when she last saw her; Dana had just not paid attention. This did not look anything like Maureen Reynolds. She looked so small, her bones so pronounced.

"Grandma," Franklin said and ran to her. He got on one knee to hug her.

Maureen closed her eyes. She lifted a hand and patted him on the back of his head.

When she opened her eyes, she looked right at Dana, who could not read the expression she saw there.

Dana felt an overwhelming need to apologize to this woman for what she had said, and for how she had said it, the last time she was here.

Maureen's lips were cracked.

Dana turned to Ness and, whispering, asked if she had any Vaseline for Maureen's lips.

"Brought that down a few minutes ago. Must have left it in the kitchen."

"Hello, Maureen," Dana said.

Reynolds holds her hand and it's a good thing because she has no impetus of her own and would just stop if he let go. But his enthusiasm is channeled down his arm and through their connected hands to her, so she leaps up the stairs with him onto the porch of his mother's house for the first time. He tells her to relax again, just as he had while they sat in the car. He was just supposed to be someone she enjoyed kissing, so why was she here?

"It's no big deal to meet my mom," he says. "Mom's met all my girlfriends. She enjoys it, so it's not a prelude to anything, necessarily."

"How many girlfriends has dear Mom met?"

"Huh?"

"You heard me."

He grins and opens the door. "Mom! Ness! We're here. Someone I'd like for y'all to meet."

"Coming," they hear from down the hallway. "Make yourselves comfortable."

The house is immaculate. The tables are old with white marble tops. She smiles at the hermetically sealed upholstered furniture. "Spills just wipe right up!" she says in a loud whisper.

He knows immediately to what she refers and laughs with his head thrown back.

They can hear rustling from someplace in the house.

She is suddenly nervous; it moves through her like a draft.

He looks at her. They kiss. The kiss reassures her, fortifies her.

"Why y'all still standing at the door? Warren. Hello, honey, I'm Maureen."

Maureen is what they call a handsome woman. Son and mother look so much alike, the same smooth, planed forehead, the large, warm eyes with the prominent cheekbones just under them. The features they have in common are more manly than feminine. They look better on Reynolds, Dana decides. Maureen is not big, but she is tall and strong looking with wide wrists and ankles. She wears a tasteful brown dress with white dots.

Warren formally introduces Maureen Reynolds to Dana Muller.

He's obviously already prepared her for the white skin; there's no shock on Maureen's face. Dana can feel she is being assessed. She frets that her skirt is too short. She is glad she did not wear a lot of makeup.

"Warren says you're going to be a teacher. What grade?"

"Yes, ma'am. I'm aiming at third through fifth. One of those."

"That's nice. That's nice. Well come on in." She gestures toward the living room and Dana follows Warren, resisting at the last second the urge to take hold of his arm.

"I like your dress, Mrs. Reynolds."

Maureen smiles and thanks Dana.

They sit on the couch, Maureen in a big wingback chair. The vinyl cries out, almost shrieks, as air is released under their weight.

At the sound, Warren looks to Dana, but she avoids his gaze, fearing she will break out in laughter. She bites her lip.

Maureen says, "It's about time I got to meet one of Warren's girlfriends. But he keeps saying, 'They not important enough for you to meet, Mama.'"

Now it is Warren who looks away. Dana can see the side of his face though. She can tell from the swell of his cheek he is grinning.

———

There was a long quiet. It was not awkward, just understandable. Minds were adjusting, feeling their way. Franklin brought up school, telling his grandmother the results of a test he had mentioned to her on his last visit.

Dana had forgotten to tell him not to mention Doug Peel or William. She hoped he wouldn't.

Ness touched Dana's arm and led her to the kitchen.

"It's the chemo and the radiation, mostly the chemo. They were too aggressive with the dosage, I guess. Her organs were shutting down."

"Oh, Ness."

Ness was rubbing her hands together just under her chin. "So they've stepped it down."

"Ness, I'm sorry."

"I have to take her in for radiation every day." Ness rapidly shook her head. "She—she...the last two or three days has started begging me not to take her. I'll say, c'mon, Mama. And she says, 'Nessie please. Please Nessie.'"

Nessie turned away.

Dana could hear her son's voice from the dining room. He was charging through a one-sided conversation. Franklin knew about mortality. Dana had explained, when he was old enough to ask, that his father was dead.

"I'm at my wit's end. They gave me a leave of absence from my job. They say they'll hold it for me. I don't know. I don't trust my boss, petty little man." She breathed out loudly. "Damned woman. Started smoking again when Warren...after the accident. Everybody she knows told her to let those things go. So shit, you know? She'd tell us she turned to Christ. Hell, she turned to tobacco."

"I haven't seen her smoke."

"You come here with Frankie, you won't. She puts 'em away for Frankie."

"Mama, Mama," Franklin called. "Grandma wants to talk to you."

Ness eyed Dana. She looked as if she wanted to say something else, but then shrugged. Dana left her in the kitchen.

So even Maureen's cancer was tied to the accident, to Dana. Dana thought, *the scariest part was when the car spun, the lack of control.* Even scarier to think you would never get the control back.

Franklin, who had been kneeling at his grandmother's side, stood when Dana returned.

The distress on his face made her want to hug him. She asked him to bring her one of the dining-room chairs. She touched his arm as he dragged the chair over for her.

He left to find Ness.

Dana scooted her chair close to Maureen's so that the arms of the two chairs touched. Dana would never have gotten this physically close to a healthy Maureen. There was a time when she would have wanted to.

The Reynolds family never fully accepted her. She adapted to her status in a distant orbit easily, without much drama. She had grown up that way. Dana's father had moped and grieved for months when Dana's mother died, or so she was told, and then he met someone and put her mother away as people do keepsakes they have no practical use for in a box on a closet shelf. Her sister claimed that the two of them were put in that keepsake box too. Eighteen months after his wife's death he married a woman with two young children, who became more important to him, Dana felt, than the two he'd already had. So her sister, Leslie, a child herself, raised Dana. But even the sisters—taking a cue from Dad, Dana supposed—had drifted apart over time.

"Maureen, I hear the doctors are working you over pretty well."

Maureen smiled. "They trying."

Dana patted the woman's wrist.

"I told Frankie to keep up his grades for me. I told him to do it if he never had another reason except he knew it would make me happy."

"Okay. I'll stay on him, but he's a good student."

She didn't look comfortable in the chair. She looked like she was fighting g-forces, like she was being pushed on. She breathed that way, too.

Maureen reached out with a suddenness that startled Dana. She grabbed Dana's nearest hand, just three fingers of it. The grasp pinched and Dana tried to adjust her hand, but Maureen maintained the awkward hold.

She said through strained breath, "Is he all right?"

Dana knew she wasn't speaking of Franklin.

"Is he hurt? Is he happy?"

———————————

"He's fine, just fine. No sign of trauma." Dana can tell the doctor, a young woman, wants her to be encouraged or invigorated by this news. Even though Dana has just been pulled from a car accident, the doctor wants something from her, wants a good trouper's smile. "Fetuses have layers of protection in the womb…"

Maureen bursts in just then. She leans to the bed. She is frantic with fear.

Dana looks to the doctor for help. Surely, it is too early for visitors. But the doctor shrinks and slips away.

The way Maureen presses against the bed hurts Dana's ribs and hip. She steels herself for the waves of pain, but they don't come.

"They won't tell me a thing. Did you see him? Is he all right? Is he hurt?" Dana blinks her eyes. The medications they gave her are seeping into her brain.

Maureen's face is close to hers. "Child," Maureen says.

Dana can see the steering wheel and the empty driver's-side seat. The driver's-side door is open wide to the perfect blackness of the bridge's shadow and the river water. The door's window is shattered.

"It's okay, child. He just went for help and got lost. He'll be here directly. Shh, shh."

Dana doesn't understand if she's being told news or being offered hope.

A hand smooths her hair.

She wants to say, "But all that water." And isn't sure if the words have come out or not. She wants to ask where is he.

She still feels the pain, but the knife isn't as sharp; it's persistent but growing duller.

"Don't cry. Don't cry."

She feels a touch. At the top of her head she is being stroked. Petted.

She sees an indistinct Maureen above her. It is amazing that the gentleness of the hand overwhelms the pain. She can close her eyes.

"Shh. Shh."

The hand touches the side of her face. She is being caressed.

From the kitchen Dana could hear Ness's and Franklin's voices in quiet conversation. With her free hand, Dana touched Maureen's cheek, then held her palm to it. She leaned in until her lips were to the woman's ear, then proceeded to tell what lies she could muster.

XVI. WHITE THIGHS

As a teacher, she had developed an ear for knowing when she was being lied to. She knew who had passed the note, if the homework had at least been attempted, and who had called who a name first. And she had known, deep down, that there was no job rebuilding a shed. Yet she'd had no choice but to let him go.

Now she would go out and find him again. It wasn't that Dana had gotten over her fear. She knew that Doug Peel was out there and that he knew where she lived. She could still see him hitting the ragged Goat Man, hear the impact of his fists on the man's face. He'd walked too close to her, leaned too close to her. And when he had interposed himself between her and her car door, preventing her from shutting it, it had been one of the most torturously long moments of her life.

Still, she had to find her husband.

She walked Franklin to Brenda's. He had not wanted to go, or maybe he had not wanted her to go, and they had a scene over it.

"Don't let him out," Dana said to her friend.

"Mine either. Who knows what a creep will do? Dana, where do you think you are going? Take Geoff, he could bark if there's trouble. He'll be home soon."

"Thanks for the offer, but I have no plans to get out of my car."

"It's getting dark fast these days. You won't see anything. Honey, can't you stay home?"

Dana patted her friend's hand, which was reaching for her. Brenda was about to say something else; her mouth opened, but Dana turned quickly and went back through the front doorway. She looked side to side, surveying the parked cars and the spaces between them before heading for her car.

She could feel the futility of her search as soon as she was three blocks away. She drove over to Serve and waited in the parking lot, too afraid to run inside and see if he was there. She kept the engine running and the doors locked and turned her shoulders every few seconds, trying to see in every direction. After ten minutes she could no longer take the vulnerable feeling that came with being stationary.

She hoped to find Jessie again. She checked behind the abandoned gas station before she went to the train station and the museum. She drove up and down streets including the street Goat Man had chased her down. The sun highlighted the clouds in orange and the sky turned purple. Nearer earth, traffic was thinning and lights were coming on in some of the windows of the homes she passed. She turned on her headlights, as most of the other cars had theirs on.

She relaxed about being followed. She had made so many turns, this way and that, and U-turns too—no one could have tailed her. But it was time to go home and talk to Franklin about his day, time to sit in front of the TV and grade papers.

She drove through the intersection where she had first spotted Reynolds holding his sign. She imagined finding him there and pulling her car to a squealing stop right in front of him, cars honking because she's holding up traffic and telling him to get in the car. *Get in the car and leave the sign,* she would say. And he would do it. And they would go home.

Two figures crossed the lot of Jessie's gas station. She had almost missed them. Dana cursed to herself and made a U-turn as soon as she could. One of the figures looked to be female.

Her tires crackled over the loose rocks of the station's seldom-used driveway. She saw no one. She drove slowly around the little station house. In the twilight, her headlights illumined the pair. They were leaning against the back wall of the station, very close together.

Jessie put her palm out to block the light and Dana switched the headlights off.

"Jessie, I've been looking for you."

"What do you want?"

From the momentary splash of the headlights, and even in the dimming twilight, Dana could see there was something wrong with Jessie's face.

"It's me, Dana." Dana climbed from her car. Dana had pepper spray, a flashlight, a big pocket knife, and a fully charged phone. She left them all on the passenger seat.

"I know who you are. I ain't dense. Get lost."

"I was wondering where you took off to the other day."

There was no reply.

Dana said, "I owe you! I owe you! That was my Reynolds. You found him."

The man behind Jessie said something. Jessie didn't respond to him.

"Told you I would."

"Let's go get something to eat."

Dana took a step forward. Jessie took a step back.

"Are you hungry? What happened to your face?"

Her lips and left cheek were swollen out of proportion. The cheek was discolored.

"Bitch, get the fuck out of here."

"Jessie."

The john would not step out from the thin shadow of the wall. He grumbled something that again Dana did not catch.

"Ain't me that's holding you up, cowboy. G'on, she likes to watch. She's watched before." She hooked her thumbs in her pants and shoved them down.

The man shifted. There was a thump—either his head or his feet hit the wall behind him. He did not reach for Jessie.

Jessie's white panties and thighs glowed in the dusk.

"C'mon, Jessie. I'll pay you more than this guy is to just come get a sandwich. C'mon, pull your pants up."

Jessie bent over, tugging at the waistband of her panties. "Come and get it, cowboy."

"I need your help, Jessie. I've lost him again. We were supposed to meet at the train station, but he didn't show. I need you."

"Bitch, what part of get the fuck lost don't you get?" Jessie took a step to the side and nearly stumbled over her pants. She caught herself with her hands spread on the broken pavement. "You told your real boyfriend that I was 'fleecing' you. You put him on me, bitch." Her hands came up from the pavement full of broken chunks of asphalt. She flung a handful at Dana.

Dana turned her face, put out a hand.

She was struck below her ear. Other pieces rattled off her car.

Jessie reared back to release the second volley. Dana's arms were up defensively. She scrambled to her car, managing to get behind the opened door just as more rocks bounced off it. Dana jumped in and closed the door after her.

"Bitch!" she heard.

She had never cut the engine. She shoved the gearshift into reverse and stomped on the gas. The car lurched back, narrowly missing the corner of the station. Dana flicked on her headlights. There was Jessie, her pants around her ankles, her white legs shining, casting about for more rocks.

Dana reversed the car all the way around the building to the front, where the gas pump used to be. She shifted back into drive.

When she touched the left side of her neck, just below her ear, she brought away dots of blood. It didn't hurt.

What did hurt was that Peel had poisoned Jessie to her. He had beaten her, too. She needed to convince Jessie to go to the police. Together they could put that bastard away.

She put the car in park and cut the lights. She looked around 360 degrees. Cars streamed by to her right. Night had completely fallen now. She knew she should get back to Franklin. And she knew she had pushed Brenda's hospitality and friendship too far. But her mind tarried there only briefly before returning to Reynolds and Peel and Jessie. She didn't want Jessie hating her. Even if she could not convince Jessie to go to the police, she wanted Jessie to know that Doug Peel had lied to her. She did another 360.

Maybe that was why Jessie had disappeared the day they found Reynolds. Had she spotted Peel watching them? It was possible. But then, if Peel had already contacted her and threatened her before, why wouldn't she say something to Dana about having met him, "her real boyfriend"?

She cut the engine. Dana shoved the knife and cell phone in her pockets. She took her pepper spray and flashlight and climbed out. She walked around the tiny building. "Jessie?" She saw nothing and then clicked on her light, shining it from side to side. They were gone. She called the woman's name several more times.

She looked behind a Dumpster, stacks of wood pallets, and through the links of the fence that protected a used car lot. She saw a few different ways Jessie and her john could have snuck away and avoided her. She heard an abrupt noise behind her and spun around. She didn't see anything, but the noise had spooked her enough to send her back toward her car. She checked to make sure she had the pepper spray nozzle pointed correctly.

It was while walking back to her car that another thought occurred to her. If Peel knew about Jessie, then he knew about Reynolds. Maybe Reynolds had intended to meet her at the train station that evening. She slung the flashlight beam in a haphazard circle around herself. She felt herself trembling. "Reynolds," she said aloud, and hurried to the car. She locked herself in.

Now she had something to dread: Reynolds had been hurt or killed by Peel. She started sobbing, her head pressed on the steering wheel. She knew she was vulnerable in the middle of a parking lot in the dark, and she wasn't being vigilant, but she didn't care.

She wasn't sure of how much time had passed, but it was long past time to go home. Franklin and Brenda would be worried sick. She fished her phone out of her pocket.

Light exploded into the car. It was so bright everything in the car turned white. Shielding her eyes with a hand, she could make out a patrol car with its floodlight trained on her. Several seconds went by and the light continued to bore into her. She thought maybe they were waiting for her to get out, but when she put a hand to the door an amplified voice said, "Please remain in your car. Put your hands on top of the steering wheel."

They made her wait what seemed an inordinate amount of time. The light was shifted.

Finally, an officer appeared at her door. He signaled for her to roll down her window. She had to turn the key in order to do so, but turned it the wrong way and the car started.

The officer banged on the window hard. "Hey. Kill the engine."

"Sorry."

She turned the key. Lowered the window.

He asked for her license and registration and told her to wait, which she thought she already had.

She wiped tears and mucus on the sleeve of her blouse.

"Ma'am, you're on private property. What are you doing here?"

Dana tried to think. She could not form the words fast enough to sound coherent.

"Ma'am, please, exit the vehicle at this time."

There was another officer. He had a flashlight and walked the lot, aiming it at the pavement.

"Mrs. Reynolds, why are you stopped here?"

"I—I'm distraught." A fresh round of tears rolled down her face. "I'm being stalked. He's hurting my friends. I filed a report with you guys."

"Did you have an encounter with this stalker tonight, Mrs. Reynolds?"

Dana shook her head.

"Bill, Mrs. Reynolds says she filed a report of being stalked with the department."

Bill walked back to the patrol car.

"In the meantime, ma'am, I'm going to give you a quick field sobriety test. If you refuse or fail, I'll ask you to take a Breathalyzer exam. You may refuse, however—"

"I won't refuse, officer."

She was made to close her eyes and touch her nose. He asked her to count to twenty using only odd numbers. She counted, "…seventeen, nineteen, twenty."

"Twenty is not an odd number."

"But you said to count to twenty. Trick question. My students would say that was a trick question." She sniffed.

Bill returned. He nodded, which Dana took to mean her story checked out.

"Okay, so why are you out here?" His voice was suddenly a lot less formal.

Dana looked at him, noticing for the first time how young he was. "Looking for a friend," she said and wiped her face with a hand, then wiped the hand on her slacks. "She's homeless, but I see her around this area sometimes. I'm worried the stalker, Doug Peel, may hurt her too. I think he already has."

"And you didn't find her?"

"Briefly, but she ran away."

Bill asked, "Are you okay to drive, ma'am?"

"Yes."

The officers looked at each other.

"I'll drive her. You follow." He returned her license and registration. When he got behind the wheel, he saw the pepper spray and had her lock it in her glove box.

The leather pouches and holster attached to his belt creaked. He pulled out his nightstick and placed it at his feet.

Dana shut the passenger door. "I live at—"

"I know where you live, Mrs. Reynolds."

On the way, he asked her about Doug Peel. She told him about the incident with Goat Man.

He would nod at her every sentence. As they pulled into the space in front of her town house, he promised he would swing by her place at least a couple of times each shift.

The patrol car pulled up behind them.

The patrolman said his name was Officer Robert Horn and he said she could ask for him since he was now familiar with her case.

Brenda and Geoff came out of the house. Geoff remained on the stoop, but Brenda came running.

Dana could hear Geoff trying in vain to call his wife back.

Robert Horn smiled at Dana. "And ma'am, you're a teacher? You should know twenty is an even number."

"Exit the vehicle, officer," Dana said.

He touched the brim of his cap. They both got out.

Brenda waited for the police car to drive away. "What's going on?" she asked.

They headed towards Brenda's door and Geoff.

"Doug Peel roughed up that homeless woman I've told you about."

"So he is dangerous."

"Oh, I knew that by the way he hit that homeless man. All he had to do was push him away. He told Jessie not to see me anymore."

"Oh, Dana."

"Come on in, you two."

"Brenda, what if he's hurt Reynolds too?"

"C'mon in."

Brenda said, "We're safe out here with you watching over us, aren't we, dear?"

"Not really." He went inside.

"How's Franklin?"

"I think he worried himself asleep, poor little guy."

"I'll get him."

"Naw." She waved a hand. "No need to move him. Let him sleep."

"You sure?"

"He's practically mine anyway."

"Thanks, Brenda. I'll tell you what happened tomorrow."

"You want to stay over too?"

"Kind of, but I'll go home. I'll be okay."

"I'll stand here til you close your door."

"Thanks, honey."

Inside, Dana kicked off her shoes and turned on the television.

She couldn't calm down. She was jittery. She missed Franklin, but was grateful he would not see her like this, and grateful she would not have to answer all his questions. She was reminded of when he was a baby and she would finally coax him to go to sleep. Even though he had worn her out, seconds after leaving his room she missed him. Franklin had enabled her to survive the last nine years. Him and practically nothing else.

She went to the powder room, pushed her hair back, and checked the spot where the rock had hit her. On her neck under her ear was a small bruise and two dots of red. Poor Jessie, the woman felt betrayed. Well, she was slightly easier to find than Reynolds; Dana would have to find her again, preferably when the woman wasn't earning some change, and explain Doug Peel to her. That crazy bastard. How had he managed to be watching her when she had no clue he was there? The first time she was searching for Reynolds, Peel and Dana had run into each other. What had he said to her? She was certain she had said nothing to encourage him. Dana tried to recall. He had been holding a newspaper over his head. Maybe he had said something about the weather. It was brief, whatever it was. It was nothing. Had that started it all for him, or did it go back further? Rationale for a stalker doesn't exist, so they say. You could confront them, but get no explanation that would satisfy. He just better stay away from Franklin. *I'll burn his eyes out with pepper spray.*

She made herself some decaf and sipped it a bit in front of the TV.

The news was on. She listened and heard none of it, but it helped her. She could not see how she could possibly sleep tonight. Her satchel was beside her on the couch and she pulled out a stack of essays. The Commonwealth of Virginia had mandated that she could not use the term "abolitionist," just "people who fought against slavery." And she couldn't say "slaves," but "enslaved people." She'd long since given up puzzling over the reasons for these mandates. The scrawl of the essay on top of the stack made her eyes hurt. Her pencil was buried somewhere at the bottom of her satchel. The papers sat on her lap.

Despite believing herself too amped up to sleep, she felt her mind shut down and her head curled to her chest.

The knocking woke her. The essays slid to the floor.

There was a knock at the door and she was certain it was Franklin, having decided he wanted to sleep in his own bed as he did sometimes, after waking up Brenda and Geoff to tell them he was leaving. Brenda would stand in her doorway in her nightgown watching the practically sleepwalking kid until he was home inside. Dana had told him if he was going to sleep over, stay the whole night; don't interrupt everyone's sleep. This time, she would tell him it was all right. Still mushy-headed from having nodded off, she flung the front door open without thinking or checking.

It was Reynolds.

He said, "There was a car accident."

XVII. VISUAL FRICTION

"Dana?"

It took her a moment.

The clean clothes she had given him were soiled and tattered. One pant leg was split and she saw blood edging the tear.

"May I come in?"

"Reynolds." She took his hand. It was all right to take his hand. She had taken it last time she'd found him. She pulled him into the house. She peeked past him to her small front yard and the street. It was dark and still. There were no lights on at Brenda's.

She shut the door behind them and locked it.

She walked right into him, buried her face in his chest, and wrapped her arms about his ribs. She had promised herself she would do that. If she ever found him again, she would not hesitate or wonder if it was all right—she would hold him and hold on to him.

After a second, his arms encircled her. They got off balance and fell against the front door but neither of them relinquished their hold on the other.

"I had trouble finding your place in the dark. I didn't remember the number."

"You found it."

Dana took a step back. His arms fell away. She tried to smile for him, but figured her face looked like a wet mess.

He moved her hair out of her face.

"Don't," she said.

He took his hand away, but all she had meant was *don't look at me, I'm a fright.*

She took the hand and squeezed it to say it was okay.

She kneeled in front of him. She pulled apart the tear on the leg of his trousers. A bit of the fabric was stuck to his leg. She pulled it away. He made a little hiss. "Sorry," Dana said, looking up at him. If it was possible, he looked worse now than he had the first time she had brought him home. There was an abrasion the size of an oblong DVD from the side of his knee to just above the knee. It was red and white where his layer of brown skin had been peeled away. *Peel.*

"What happened?"

"Like I said, there was a car accident, but I didn't have a car. Some fool in a great hurry hit me. Maybe he was playing let's-scare-the-bum, but got too close."

"People do that? This is fresh. This just happened?"

"On my way over here. Well, while I was hunting for the place. I was a couple of blocks over. And yeah, people do that. It doesn't count if you're mean to people who don't count."

"I don't think it was an accident. I don't think it was random."

"He sideswiped two parked cars. I checked them. There's going to be some pissed owners in the morning. No car alarm went off, though. That's not where I got hit."

He raised his shirt and coat. On his side, above his hip, was a large bruise.

Dana touched it.

"The side rearview mirror got me right there."

"Reynolds…"

"I think he'd been parked just a half-block up or so. Anyway, he came tearing directly at me. But the fool didn't have his lights on. So I figure he doesn't see me and hop out of his path. I didn't expect him to swerve right at me. I barely got out of the way. The side mirror got me here. My hand hit something too. It's sore. The impact picked me up and when I hit the pavement I skidded on that knee."

"Did you get a look at the driver?"

"Not even a little bit. Car neither. Sedan. Couldn't even tell you the color." He seemed calm, yet his hands kept moving.

"I'm going to fix you up, okay?"

"I believe you could."

The bathrooms in Dana's town house were tiny. He sat on the toilet seat lid and she sat on the edge of the bathtub and tended to his abrasion—"road rash," he called it.

She used scissors to cut up the ruined pant leg. "That's not so bad," she told him after more closely inspecting the wound. She wiped the area with cotton balls soaked in rubbing alcohol. He winced and cursed on cue. Tiny black particles from the street came up. She showed him the dirty cotton with the pieces of asphalt.

"You could rub me anywhere and get that much dirt."

She smiled. "God, Reynolds, the black is finally coming off."

"Hah!"

His smile warmed her out of all proportion.

Her left hand rested on his knee. Looking at him, she saw the bristles and wires sprouting from his face and head. He still had the wild man look. For a moment, she did not see her Reynolds in all that wildness. "We—we'll get you a shower. Reynolds, do you remember the first time I persuaded you to let me cut your hair?"

He smiled at her. Whether at the memory or the question, Dana did not know.

"Reynolds, did you get amnesia? Do you remember everything?"

He looked away, perhaps at his reflection in the mirror. "I remember enough," he said. "Too much."

Don't push him, Dana thought. *He's here; just take care of him.* She stood. They were in cramped quarters. Her legs were against his left arm. Her hands hesitated a moment and then slowly lighted on his face, which she could see in the mirror. His eyes closed when her hands made contact. She gently brushed back the hair from his face. The hair on his cheeks and chin was coarse, the hair on his head soft and unruly, springing back with its own will each time she lifted her hand. "There was no shed to repair, was there?"

His eyes opened. He was looking at her reflection. "No."

"Doesn't matter. I'm glad you came back."

He takes his two middle fingers and brushes back her hair. His face is a hand's width from hers and their eyes are locked. He doesn't kiss her on the lips, as she expects, but on the cheek, and so gently it burns through her. That is not a goodnight-at-the-door kiss; it is a prelude kiss, a promise.

She had told a friend, and herself, that his skin color was not a factor, that it did not matter. But it did. She loves the contrast of their complexions, the visual friction. Loves his deep brown. It is a turn-on, a waning but lingering taboo that excites her. She wonders if that is wrong, but it's her secret.

She performs a quick inventory; her legs are shaved, she has on cute underwear, and the bedroom isn't too horribly a mess.

The second kiss is between her eyebrows. His breath warms her face. She tries to swallow. "Do you want to come in?"

The third kiss is on her lower lip and there is gentle pressure, which she returns. And then he whispers, "Yes."

She places a hand on her doorknob. It doesn't turn. "Where's my keys? Let me find my goddamn keys!"

"Take your coat off," she said.

He winced while freeing his arms of the sleeves.

"Hold this arm up."

She stooped, lifted the arm herself, and then lifted the shirt to look at the bruise left by the car's mirror. She lightly touched it with the pads of two fingers. She didn't know why, but then decided she was checking to see if there was any broken bone. She said, "The skin's not broken."

"Hurts like a sonovabitch."

"We should take you to the emergency room."

"Hmmm. And me with my insurance lapsed."

"I'll pay, silly," Dana said, wondering where the money would come from.

"Thanks. No."

"Too cold."

She stood, returned to his hair, touching it idly. "I'm going to cut your hair. You have enough here for everybody and the little boy who lives down the lane."

"Are you calling my hair wool?" He was looking at her in the mirror.

"Guess I am. It's woolly." There being no objections, she shoved things around under the sink until she found her clippers. "Any time Halley's Comet appears, Franklin lets me cut his hair whether he needs it or not." She added, "He's a good boy."

"I can tell. Where is he? I wanted to see him. Talk comics."

"Sleeping next door with friends." She plugged in the clippers. She tried to rake the hair with her fingers, but it was too tangled. She found matted hair, too, and said nothing.

"I'll be right back."

She went into her bedroom and found newspaper.

At the bathroom door she asked, "Do you want something to drink? Something to eat?"

He'd been looking at himself in the mirror. "Yes, later though, Dana."

She spread the newspaper on both sides of the toilet, tapped his feet, and put a sheet under them when he lifted them.

"We're set." She switched on the clippers. A loud hum filled the little room.

He held up a finger. "I've been wounded enough tonight," he said.

"Oh, shush."

"Do I have a say in what style cut I get?"

"Not really, no."

It was quiet in the bathroom after that except for the varying hum of the clippers. The air was cool in the little room; the seasons were changing and Dana had not turned on the heat. Her bare feet were cold on the tiles. Reynolds remained still, unlike the fidgety Franklin, who made each hair a moving target.

He submitted to her without resistance, allowing her to shift his head in any direction she wished. It seemed to require more closeness than a kiss—maybe not as intimate, but more familiar, touching his temples, folding back an ear, holding the curve of his head.

The hair fell. She brushed it from his neck and shoulders. The shirt needed washing anyway. The newspaper looked like a battlefield, the hair twisted and curled in defeat.

She cut the hair short, not quite shaved. There was grey, actually white, at his temples and above the ears. She touched the colorless hairs with a finger. She gave him a hairline all around, experiencing a little trouble getting it even in the back. He was patient through all her minor adjustments.

She caught him studying her in the mirror. Their eyes met and neither broke away from the gaze. In the mirror, Dana could see the smile on her face. His face wasn't smiling. His eyes looked a little tired. "The whiskers have to go. You look like a caveman from one of those insurance commercials."

"I don't know what you're talking about; my TV's on the fritz. But isn't this a full-service establishment? Where's the management?" He looked around. Made to get up.

Dana pushed down on his shoulders. "Do you want a short beard or can I take it all off?"

He hesitated, exhaled loudly, and said, "Take it off."

"Good!" she said.

He took one of her hands and held it against his chest. "Just savoring," he said and let his hand slowly slip away from hers.

Dana was soaring. She felt heat from that hand. She turned from the mirror. She got her shaving cream and her little pink disposable razor, which, considering his thick beard, seemed like a butter knife about to be used to carve a turkey.

"You use that on my beard and it'll just get lost in there."

"I'll be like, where'd it go?"

"Days later, it falls out in my soup."

They laughed. She rested a hand briefly on his shoulder. She wanted to sit in his lap. Her leg muscles actually twitched from the unsanctioned command. She used to sit in Reynolds's lap; they would talk that way sometimes, faces inches apart.

"The clippers first then."

The sculpting continued. The wiry hair fell away, covered the backs of her hands. "Doesn't this stuff itch?" she asked. He grunted. She was careful around his lips. She lifted his chin to get beneath it.

Then she applied the shaving cream, using way more than needed, giving him a white foam beard.

"What are you doing?" There was that amused, crooked smile.

"Santa." *Now maybe I could sit on your lap.* She grinned at the thought, wondered what his reaction would be, but did not do it.

She shaved him very carefully, his face slowly emerging with each stroke. She cleaned the razor frequently in the running tap. She appraised the smooth, newly exposed skin before making each stroke, leaning her face whisper-close to his. She could hear the water running and the scraping of the blade over cheeks and chin.

She kept her face close, seeing pores and nostrils, but saved viewing the whole face until she was done. When she'd rinsed the razor for the last time, set it aside, and turned off the tap, she stepped back.

He raised his face to hers.

Dana stopped like slamming on brakes and feeling all that momentum lurch wildly and bowl you over. She must have stared at the face for a long time. She compared it to every memory she ever had. Just two, maybe three years after he had disappeared, she had been amazed at how quickly the memories began to fade, how difficult it was to hold images in your head that time had decided you no longer needed. It had been true of Franklin too. The images of him as a baby, no longer than her forearm, suckling at her breast, lying on his back reaching for the dangling mobile—all faded. The knowledge doesn't go, the feelings don't go, and they are what tease you and coax you to form the photograph in your head that just won't completely develop. And now it had been nearly ten years and she began to understand just what a feat she had performed on a clouded rainy night by only the light of headlights and a traffic light, to see through a tangle of hair and the fog of a decade to recognize Warren Reynolds.

For all those minutes she had been examining him, he must have been looking at her just as intently. "You can see it now? I am not your Reynolds?"

"What?" Dana looked away. There were bits of this man's hair on the backs of her hands.

"How long has it been, Dana?"

She turned on the tap and started washing her hands. "Ten years."

She turned off the water, grabbed a towel. She backed away until she hit the doorway frame, six feet away from him and as far as she could get in the tiny bathroom.

"The man you're looking for couldn't possibly still exist."

She wiped her eyes with the towel.

"After you take a shower and wash all that hair off, we'll bandage your knee and I'll find you some clothes."

XVIII. THE NEW NORMAL

She feels more than just a little silly. But she feels he has visited her, communicated with her at last. She's never believed in such things, never bought into that guy on TV who talks to people who have crossed over. Dana looks back at her car. She found a spot on the shoulder of the road where she could park well away from traffic, but still she worries and looks back repeatedly. Her baby is in there, strapped in his carrier, belted to the back seat. She doesn't believe in spirits now, either, or those "sensitive" people who claim to have heard from them. She prefers to act on what she felt without examining it too closely. She has to look down; there are a lot of loose gray rocks that could roll her ankles. Every few seconds a car zips by. The breeze they create tugs at her clothes and the cheap grocery store bouquet of flowers she holds, and she looks back at the car, imagining she can see the sleeping Franklin within it. She is almost to the bridge, which doesn't look so imposing from the top, in daylight. The new guardrail makes her stop for a moment. It is made of shiny new steel and has diagonal yellow bands painted on it every yard or so. *Too late*, she thinks and avoids the temptation to step closer and peek down the steep embankment dropping away behind the rail.

She's not prepared for the wind. A chill hits her as soon as she steps on the hard pavement of the bridge. It must be channeled by the trees on either side of the river's banks, and surges full bore over the water. Dana pulls herself in, wraps her arms tightly, and checks the petals of the flowers. Well, she is here now, feeling cold as well as silly. The water does not look deep at all, but it had been raining that night and almost every day the week prior and the river had been swollen. And she was told there are shelves and drop offs in there. But, still. The idea that he was lodged between rocks down there is horrible, so horrible she gasps and pushes the image out of her mind. She looks back at the car. She can't see it well now; the walk was farther than she thought and the road has a subtle curve to it and hides the bottom half of her car. She wants to hurry now. Maternal dread pulls at her. If she simply lets go of the flowers, the wind would whip them into the bridge or over her head into traffic. They would end up on some trucker's windshield. She looks down at the pavement around her, then jogs back to the shoulder of the road and collects several rocks, which she pushes into the bouquet's paper cone. She stops there. She can see the bridge stretch away from her in the hard brightness. She turns and almost breaks into a run toward her car and her baby. On the way, she shakes the rocks from the flowers.

———————

Outside of the bathroom, in her bedroom, she sat on the edge of her bed and buried her face in her hands. The voice had seemed right. His height. His shoulders…the eyes.

She dammed her own eyes by pushing the heels of her palms into them. The light from the bathroom doorway was the only light on. Now she had a stranger outside waiting on her and a stranger inside. She would have to warn him about Peel. She was convinced Peel had already tried to run him over and would wait for another opportunity to strike again.

She jumped up abruptly. She went through the boxes in the guest room closet and pulled out more of Reynolds's clothes. She shook them out and then refolded some. He was in the shower when she returned to the bathroom. She sat the clothes on the vanity near the sink.

———————

He pulls her into the spray and soaps her, gliding the bar and his hands over her skin, until their bodies slide against each other. She tastes the water rolling down his chest.

———————

"Some clean clothes here," she said and left. She heard his thank you shouted over the falling water.

Heading downstairs, she realized she did not know the name of the man in her shower. She put on link sausages and got out bread and eggs. Later, she would make up the sofa with a pillow, sheets, and a blanket.

Doug Peel was out there, sitting behind the wheel of his side-scraped car with a broken driver's-side rearview. He would be seething.

She was facing the stove when "Reynolds" entered the kitchen.

"I followed the scent," he said.

"I'm making breakfast," she said without turning around. She poured the eggs onto the hot skillet. "Because that's all that I have ready to eat."

"Fine, and thank you."

The skillet was hot; the eggs cooked quickly.

"I don't know your name." She turned around, unprepared to see the man sitting at her kitchen table, his elbows on his knees. Her breath caught. Maybe it was the clothes. He was wearing a long-sleeved Henley and dark blue pants she distinctly remembered seeing Reynolds in many times. She should have picked something else, something less Reynolds.

The eggs and skillet nearly dropped from her hands.

He moved to help her, but she caught it, giving herself a light burn on one finger in the process. She returned the skillet to the stove and, unconsciously, sucked the burnt finger.

"You okay, Miss?"

"What did you call me?"

He shook his head, not understanding.

"My husband used to call me Miss or Young Miss. I finally got him to stop; I always saw it as him calling me young and immature: 'Okay, Young Miss, have it your way.'"

Dana put the food on the table, then plates and forks and napkins.

Once she put the breakfast on her plate all energy for it and interest was gone. "I think I have orange juice."

"Too late for OJ, all that acid. Water? Please."

She sat the glass in front of him and sat back down. She watched him eat. She picked out the ways he was like Reynolds and the ways he wasn't, the parts that were Reynolds and the parts that were not. She decided she should be angry with this man. After all, he could have told her right away she had the wrong man, sorry, lady, and walked away. And certainly, he did not have to come back to her place tonight.

"Why did you come back? Why did you come back to the crazy woman's house? More money, food...?"

He scraped his fork across the plate, herding the eggs. "Don't be angry, Dana," he said in a soothing way. "I meant no harm." He wiped his mouth. "I guess I did come to take advantage, though not for money or food. Thank you for the food, by the way."

"I don't think I have a nickel in this house," Dana said. "I'm a teacher."

"Crazy is the new normal. Who can see what goes on in the world, or just on the streets, let alone all the crap in their own lives, and not go crazy? Living and not going crazy is like swimming and not getting wet."

"You didn't answer—"

"To be your Reynolds, if I could. To get that reception that you gave Reynolds. It wasn't meant for me, but for your Reynolds. I know that. But what a homecoming Reynolds got. Hugged, cleaned, fed, a place at the kitchen table, comic books, a bright-eyed boy, clean clothes, no questions..."

"The questions were coming."

"Hah. Yeah."

"And I have questions for you too. Like, what's your story, I mean, why are you out there? Why don't you go home? I want to know why someone would go missing, leave their family, wife, mother, sister, son."

"You want to know why." He put his hand over his mouth and looked down at the table.

Dana did not think he would answer. "You want more? You can have mine, I'm not hungry and my stomach reacts violently to changes in its feeding schedule." She pushed her plate toward him. He took the fork that she had used before she could stop him.

"Since I'm not Reynolds, by mutual agreement, can't I be William?"

"What's wrong with the name you were born with?"

"I used it up."

"What does that mean?"

"I'm wanted. By the long arm of the law." He shoveled the rest of the food in his mouth.

Dana thought this revelation should make her nervous, but she wasn't. He was disarming. There was the intelligent, obviously educated way he spoke, and that he still looked like her Reynolds. She needed to convince herself that he was a total stranger, and that she was alone in a house with a total stranger.

"Assault and robbery. Separate incidents. Don't worry. I committed the crimes, but I'm not a criminal."

"Oh. I didn't know there was a difference between, um, crime committers and criminals."

"Huge."

"What…"

"Attitude."

Dana gave him a skeptical smile. How could she explain this to Ness and Brenda? They would think her crazy—the new normal according to some. But then, Dana thought, what is there to explain? They already thought she was crazy.

"The law doesn't really allow for lapses in judgment. I don't expect you know what I mean…?"

Lapses in judgment. "I know what you mean…William."

"It doesn't make for a great defense. Lapse in judgment, Your Honor. You don't want to hear my story anyway. You want to hear Reynolds's story."

The kitchen chair was getting hard. Dana shifted. "We need to make up the couch for you."

"Tell me what happened. I can tell you his story."

"Let's get some sheets and a blanket; I'll make up the couch." Dana stood, but he did not. "'William,' I don't care to hear your theory on a man you profess to know nothing about. I don't want generalities and speculation. I need the blow by blow, the real thing."

After a pause, he said, "I didn't want you thinking your Reynolds had left you again. So I thought, I'll come back…let her have her happy ending. We could have some kind of, I don't know, more friendly parting. Then, I thought that was cruel too, because what if she stops looking for him, her husband? That wouldn't be right. Maybe it's the hope, the possibility you need. Then I thought maybe you should stop. Maybe you've been searching for a long time and need to move on, as they say. It wasn't all selfish."

"I haven't been looking long."

He shrugged, scooted his chair back, but still made no move to rise. He was looking down at his feet, at his worn, dirty sneakers. Reynolds's shoes did not fit him.

"You have."

Dana sat back down, feeling as if a wave of weariness had hit her. She had told Maureen that she had seen her son. That he was working his way back into all their lives.

"Shit," she whispered.

"What?"

"I've done mean things."

It was quiet for a long time. They sat not far apart at all. The refrigerator hummed. The fluorescent light buzzed. It was getting cool in the house. It was time to flip the thermostat to heat. Then go to bed. Get Franklin in the morning. She should have picked a different shirt for "William"—that one Reynolds had worn a lot and always looked casually and effortlessly sexy in it. Maybe she could find another shirt for him, two or three, and get this one back.

"He didn't just say one night that he was going to 7-Eleven for a pack of cigarettes or something and never came back. It wasn't like that, you know. There was an accident. An accident that was my fault. The car—we went into the river, and then he was gone."

It looked as if he was reaching for her hand. Dana snatched her hand away. She tucked both in her lap.

"You were driving?"

"No, but it was my fault." Dana felt a surprising bit of anger rise.

"I understand." He put his palms, etched with dark cracks, out toward her.

Dana got up this time. "I'll get those sheets." She went upstairs to the linen closet and got sheets and an old, warm blanket that she turtled under in the cold months while watching TV. She took one of the pillows from her bed and put a fresh pillowcase on it.

Pajamas would have been nice, but Reynolds did not wear them, just boxers and T-shirts to bed. She was glad he was here tonight; more than ever, she had the sense that Doug Peel was nearby.

William was still at the kitchen table with his elbows on his knees when she returned.

"C'mon," she said.

She led him to the living room and the sofa. She had just one shaded lamp on. "You can watch TV for as long as you care to tonight. The remote is around here somewhere." She gathered schoolwork she had abandoned on the sofa and placed the papers on a chair.

They unfolded the sheets and unfurled them like hammocks and settled them onto her long couch. "I've fallen asleep here many times. It might sleep better than my old mattress."

"Thank you. It looks better than a grate or somebody's garage and some newspapers."

"Then why don't you go home, huh, William? Why don't all of you, who aren't complete mental defectives or winos, just go the fuck home?"

"Who told you there was a home to go to? And who says I'm not a mental defective?"

"The new normal?"

She handed him the pillow and he smelled it with his eyes closed.

"Do you know what keeps a person on the street? Fear. Fear they can never return, that they've been gone too long, that each day away is like another brick in a wall that's made it that much worse, and now—whenever the now is—it is way too late and the wall is way too high. Fear of the welcome they'd receive, the blame, the guilt. That look they would get when the door opens. Fear there's nothing to return to.

"You know how you have a friend or a dad who smokes and you say, those things are killing you, why don't you stop, can't you stop, or at least try? And they say, I could stop if I wanted to, I just don't want to. What the nonsmoker can see that the smoker can't is that the 'want to smoke' is not owned by him. The want that he thinks is his is actually the addiction, yet it has all the feel of conscious choice. That's living on the street. That's the want. But instead of addiction it's fear. The too-late fear." Dana took a moment to absorb what he said before replying.

"I was in DC not long ago and saw a gentleman standing on the corner having the most animated and violent argument. I mean, his arms were going this way and that." Dana imitated him. "Spit flying. 'You told me. You said it. That's not right.' He was pointing and stabbing with his finger. And he was all by himself. Well, to all of us walking by he looked to be all by himself."

"And Dana, in a lot of cases, there isn't a home to go back to."

"Is that what you think in your case?"

He sat down, still holding the pillow against his chest. "Who was it who said, 'you can't go home again?' You're a teacher, who said that?"

"Why do people think teachers are walking encyclopedias?"

"Excuse me."

"Thomas Wolfe. Did you ever try to go home?"

"Dana," he whispered.

She took it as remonstration. She thought about saying she was sorry to be prying, but she wanted to know. Why would someone just wander away? Then she thought, in Reynolds's case, she already knew the answer.

She sat down next to him. His resemblance to her lost husband grew just as she was fighting to believe there was none. She wondered what Maureen and Ness would think. She resisted the impulse to put her forehead against his shoulder, if he could prop her up just this evening...

"I wanted to ask you, do you know Jessie?"

He frowned.

"Jessie. The woman I was with at Serve. When I found you—when we first met. She's a fortysomething, I guess, dark hair, white..."

"I think I remember the woman you were with. I didn't recognize her, though."

"Oh. She said she knew you. She pointed you out."

He shrugged, showed her empty palms.

The man on Wisconsin Avenue whom she had seen arguing to the air was convinced someone was standing right there, listening. Maybe this doppelganger of Reynolds wasn't here either. Maybe, Dana thought, she was alone in the house, finally certifiable, a crazy woman without witnesses, confessing to the air.

XIX. STEALING ELECTRICITY

This ghost took her hand, laid his hand over hers resting on the couch between them, then curled his fingers around it.

Dana looked at the hands, his around hers.

"You know, your husband, he was probably hurt bad, physically, I mean. You said there was an accident, right? There you go. See, when he left the scene, he was completely out of it, concussed and unable to think straight."

"Well, maybe at first…"

"No, listen." He turned toward her. Their eyes met for a moment. He looked as if he were pleading and she kept quiet. "If he was hurt badly he may have been walking around nearly unconscious for days. Maybe he took a ride from somebody who happened to see him. By the time he was better, his judgment was still off, made decisions with a brain that was still damaged.

"Don't look so skeptical, Dana. Something similar happened to me. I was in a fight. The assault I told you they wanted me on. The other guy had a bat and got in some good swings before I knew what was going on. Messed up my nose and mouth and one cheek with one hit and another cracked my shoulder, and then another gave me a concussion. Thing is, I won the fight. Took the bat from him and gave him better than he'd given me. That's the part of the fight people saw."

"You were arrested?"

He shook his head.

Her teacher's alarm had gone off again. There was a lie in there somewhere. She wasn't sure which part.

"I fell in with this couple. I met her first and she took me home to her apartment. This was in Baltimore. There was a man passed out on her couch and she said don't pay any attention to him. But that was her husband or so he sometimes claimed. And the apartment wasn't theirs. I didn't find that out for months. It was an abandoned building and they had set up shop. Had electricity coming in a window from somewhere with one of those long orange extension cords. They were freaks. He worked at night, stealing, with some other guy, who'd come and get him. When he'd leave he'd say to me, take care of her, talking about his wife. Take care of her, he'd say and laugh and she would laugh too.

"He took me with him a few times. We stole copper tubes, pipes from a construction site once. We took a TV and a commercial mixer from the kitchen of a restaurant. I don't remember what else.

"We'd drink. Do drugs. At night, I'd be with her, she'd be passed out next to me, and I'd ask myself what the hell I was doing. Long damn nights of thinking and rethinking. And wondering if I'd gone too far away. But I didn't think I had anything to come back to. They were filthy people and I was right in there with them. I thought about leaving them every hour of every day. I told them, told her, they were dirty people and they would laugh. They'd laugh 'cause they could see what I couldn't. They knew I was hollerin' at myself. One day she brought a boy home, a teenager, eighteen, nineteen, I don't know, a thin but scary-looking kid. She told me I had to go. I was angry. I shoved her against the door. She just laughed like she always did, but the two men were on me quick. They punched me and threw me down the stairs. All the times I thought about leaving them, and to finally let her kick me out.

"I went down the alley and saw that cord, the one they used to steal electricity with. And I followed it. It was hidden behind leaves and bricks and run down a manhole and back up the next manhole and under a fence to a storage lot where it was plugged into a light socket. I unscrewed it and took a rock and beat the plug to uselessness."

"Not too hard to repair, is it?"

"No."

"Did you ever think about the people who were wondering where you were? If you were hurt or sick? Did you wonder how they were doing? If they needed you?"

"Oh, no. I thought about them every day, every block, every step across the street. I don't know how much of my thinking back then was caused by the injury. That's what I want to tell you. Head injuries can change your personality, how you figure things, how you talk."

"Oh, I've heard that. You're right," Dana said. She did not want to argue with him or show her exasperation. She slipped her hand from his. She had not worn her wedding band for a couple of years now. Her co-workers convinced her it was keeping potential suitors away. For a while after the accident, she had worn it because it still felt right, then later so people wouldn't assume Franklin was conceived out of wedlock; they received enough second looks as it was, the white woman and her light-brown baby.

"Each day makes it harder to change, to go back. Can't really explain it better than that. You think about how they will never understand, how angry they will be. And worse, you figure ways that everybody is better off if you just stay away, how relieved they must be inside. You convince yourself that anyone you might have left is better off without you."

"You've done a number on yourself."

He stood quickly. "I had help." He flipped the pillow at her.

Dana let the pillow slide down her legs to the carpet.

He went to the front window, roughly separated the slats of the blind, and looked out. He couldn't have seen much: the street lamp across the lot, the dark windows of the other town houses, parked cars.

"I talk too much. I should go."

He stood with his back to her and Dana waited for him to return to the couch. She thought about him and the freak, the laughing woman who brought men home. And she thought of his feeble gesture with the extension cord. She wanted to call to him, but William wasn't really his name and it sounded silly to use it.

She remembered she had not bandaged his leg. "We have to see to your leg," she said. The dim room made things easier to say.

"I'm feeling antsy. It's time to go. The leg is fine."

"We don't want blood spots on the clean pants," she said.

"Fuck the pants. They're not mine. None of this is."

Dana put the pillow back on the couch. She found the remote and turned on the TV and lowered the volume to ant-like sounds.

He came back to the couch.

"I'll let you get some sleep now."

She started up the stairs. Without looking back to him, she said, "I absolutely hate the idea of his body in that river. Choked on dirty, gritty water. The fish…"

It didn't seem as if he would reply and she continued up the steps, then heard, "Naw, that's okay. Sailors bury at sea. Earth or sea, dirt or water is the same. The body eventually becomes part of the whole again anyway, right?"

Dana locked her bedroom door behind her. She went to her bathroom. He had picked up all the newspaper. His torn pants were stuffed in the trashcan. The towels he had used were folded, though they were damp. She unfolded them and tossed them over the shower-curtain rod. She used the toilet and then took a very quick shower.

She put on a stretched-out T-shirt and panties and slipped under her sheets. There would be no sleep tonight. She couldn't believe how wide awake her mind was, spinning like the Tasmanian Devil, first in one direction and then another. She lay in the dark, eyes open. Ideas and images pressed upon her. They popped up, each one as if she had just turned a corner and was hit in the face with them. She tried taking deep breaths to suppress these thoughts.

Her heart bumped against her breastbone. What she knew now scared and thrilled her. What had he said? "A dream too lovely."

She should have stayed down there and insisted on taping his leg. A strong woman would have. Ness would have. Brenda would have. *Boy, you'd better get over here and let me see to that leg. I'm not playing with you.* He might think more of her then.

She was afraid he would leave. She would go downstairs in the morning, hearing noise, but it would be Franklin returning. On the couch the sheets and blanket would be folded and stacked as the towels had been in the bathroom. She reviewed his story and his explanation of why he had stayed away, stayed on the streets for so long. She got out of bed and unlocked her bedroom door. She tried to do it silently. She left it a quarter open so she could listen for couch springs, or for the front door latch clicking.

She went back to her bed, but could hear nothing. She slipped out of the bedroom finally and sat at the top of the stairs.

He was coming out of the powder room. The television was turned off. The couch took his weight again. He turned over. This eavesdropping was wrong, but she just knew he would try to leave. Sitting there listening in the middle of the night—she was being stalkerish. *Doug Peel.*

She had not warned "William" about Peel, who had already tried to run him over.

She got to her feet and hurried down the stairs.

She whispered in the dark, "Reynolds. Reynolds."

She successfully navigated around her coffee table, which earlier she had pushed away from the couch a bit, while spreading out his sheets.

She could see a large shape on the couch. She eased herself down next to it.

She felt his warmth against her leg. His breathing was rough and loud. "Hey," she said.

She put a hand to his shoulder.

"What!" He came up quickly. His face bumped her shoulder.

"I'm sorry. It's me."

"Dana? Oh, what time is it?"

"I forgot to tell you something important. And I was afraid you would leave."

A hand brushed over her leg. He was trying to sit up. Dana didn't give him any room. She propped an elbow to the back of the couch and hovered over him.

His head, shoulders, and upper chest were visible to her now.

"Listen," she said. "The man who tried to run you over wasn't just some random homeless hater. His name is Doug Peel and I think he's a stalker. He latched on to me at some point while I was out looking for you. Apparently, he's been watching me ever since. He's approached Franklin..."

"He has?"

"...and he hit Jessie, the homeless woman I asked you about. If you leave, he could come after you again."

"You think he's out there now?"

"I'm pretty sure he used to hang out in my backyard at night."

"Did he hurt Franklin?"

"No."

"Has he hurt you?"

"No."

"All right."

"He's a white guy with black hair—some of it falls into his face like bangs and the rest he combs over because he's going bald. He's shorter than you, but stocky and..."

"Okay."

"Okay?"

"Okay, I'm forewarned."

"Well, I didn't want you leaving without knowing, and crossing a street, whistling a jig, and getting run over."

He made a little *hmph* sound.

She supposed it was time to go back upstairs and let him sleep through what remained of the night, but she did not move. Through her side, her ribs and her upper thigh, she could feel him breathing.

He placed a hand on her leg. Dana made no move to push it away. Maybe he meant to calm or comfort her.

The hand slowly moved up her leg.

"Does your side hurt? Where the mirror caught you?"

He was caressing her, describing tiny, gentle circles along her skin. "A little."

The hand came off her leg and encircled her wrist. He pulled her toward him.

"Let go," Dana said. She managed to keep her voice calm. "Let go." She tugged her arm back and he relinquished his hold.

"I'm sor—"

"Scoot over," she said. "You're hogging the whole couch." She found the edges of the sheet and blanket and pulled them back. Fine blue zigzags of static electricity crackled down the blanket as she slid in. She stretched to her length beside him and brought the sheet and blanket down over her.

The heat immediately enveloped her. He was naked. A dark arm went about her and pulled her tight against him. He smelled of her soap. They were on their sides facing each other in contact all along their bodies: legs and stomachs and chests, noses and lips. Her toes flirted with his shins. She brushed his nose with hers.

They wrestled her T-shirt off, giggling at the surprising difficulty involved, then went still again, marveling at the sensation of skin on skin. His hand was at her back, pinning her to him. Her hands caressed his chest. He nibbled under her chin and along her jaw, nuzzled at her ear.

Dana closed her eyes and gave herself over to what she wanted at the moment. She let out contented, encouraging moans. They kissed. He moved over her and his weight pushed her into the cushions. She ran her hands over his freshly cropped head. He worked her panties down and she wiggled out of them and tried kicking them away, but they remained encircling one ankle. On the tight confines of the couch, it took small adjustments and a bit more effort to get comfortably situated.

XX. VODKA

She felt him trembling against her as if he were cold. The trembling stopped and started and stopped.

"Did I take all the blanket?" she whispered.

"Dana, have you got a little something to drink in the house?" He didn't whisper. His voice was harsh right next to her ear and sounded strained.

"Vodka maybe. Brenda and I discovered White Russians—" She immediately regretted mentioning the drink, because it made her think of milk, and of the milk carton standing on the kitchen table that day long ago.

"I could use a taste. Can you get it?"

"Oh. Sure." She slipped quickly from the sheets. She nearly tripped on her panties, tried putting them on, but fumbled it and just kicked them across the room. Chilled by the air, guided by the glowing, digital numbers of the microwave, she padded to the kitchen, a little embarrassed to be naked before him.

"How do you want it?" She opened cabinet after cabinet.

"Dana."

"What?" She didn't turn on the lights. Didn't think of it until after she had found the bottle, 80 percent full.

"Straight's fine."

She grabbed a glass and returned to the couch. "I'm cold," she said as she poured.

He took the glass from her. She heard him swallow.

"Is it too early for a drink or too late?"

She said, "Either way." She was calculating the implications of this, realizing she had instantly decided it did not matter, not to her.

"A little bit more."

She poured another. This one he sipped more slowly, but it still held his attention exclusively.

"Is there more?"

She poured again.

He put an arm about her. After a couple of sips, he reached past her and set the empty glass on the coffee table.

He tried to pull her back on the couch, and though she was cold and uncomfortable sitting on the edge of it, she resisted.

He relented, but said nothing.

A minute passed with Dana holding the vodka bottle. She wondered if she should return it to the kitchen, hide it somewhere. Finally, she set it on the table next to his glass. She was about to slip back next to him when he asked, "Do you have a boyfriend?"

"No."

"How many boyfriends have you had since Reynolds left?"

"How many…what a question to ask. None of your business would be the right answer."

He held out the sheet for her.

Lying beside him again, she began to feel better. He played with her breasts, circling a finger around a nipple.

"Dating again after having been married is the worst. It is. It's like you're a college graduate, but you have to take high school English again."

He chuckled.

She watched his skating fingers.

"Three boyfriends in ten years. One was only for two months; he's the one I liked the best. He was the first one. Franklin was three. And then Mr. Corvette, don't recall his name, lasted an amazing six months. He was a lawyer. That was just a few months, or maybe it was a year, after the first one. And then I broke up from a two-year off-and-on thing just last winter before Christmas. Always break up before the holidays so you don't have to buy that extra present. Just a tip for you."

"Hmm. Who did the breaking up? You or them?"

"Let's see. The first one, he did. The second one, mutual. And maybe I did the third one."

"Ah. What did he do wrong?"

"It's going to be your turn to answer more questions after this. Let's see, he didn't do anything wrong. Decent guy. Got along with Franklin. He liked baseball. Franklin likes Harry Potter and superheroes."

"Did you ever see other guys while dating him? You know, creep out on him?"

"No. Screw you. Why would you ask that?" She hit him, couldn't say where the undirected blow landed, and pushed away. She was on her feet.

"Just making conversation."

"Screw you."

"You already have."

She put an arm across her breasts and used the free hand for a fig leaf. "The vodka's on the table. Pace yourself, 'William'; it's all I have in the house." Dana ran up the stairs.

In her bedroom, she remembered her panties were down there on the living room floor somewhere. She was in no mood to fetch them now, but wanted to retrieve them before Franklin came home and found them.

She sat on her bed, then popped up again after a second. *Did I cheat?* A question Reynolds might ask. *Man, he gave himself away with that one.* She went to the bedroom doorway. "William," she shouted down the stairs. She wasn't calling him; she was reminding him.

She stomped to her chest of drawers and jerked open the top drawer. She wasn't sure why she was angry. She fished out a set of yellow cotton pajamas and snapped them on. They had long sleeves and knee-length pants. She knew she deserved whatever bitterness he might want to sling her way.

He couldn't be wanted by the police, she suddenly thought. If he were, they would have his name and he wouldn't be officially missing or dead anymore.

"Did I cheat…"

She launched herself across her bed and landed with a bounce. It wouldn't be long until daylight now and she hadn't slept one second. She was getting less pissed by the second and more concerned. *Just don't let him leave*, she told herself. The tingly warmth from their lovemaking returned. She stanched any reflection on how stupid and how dangerous that had been. A homeless alcoholic. God! Then she thought of all the sex partners the electricity thief must have had. Stupid Dana. She tried to turn her attention to tomorrow. Franklin would come through the door and see that the man had returned. There was so much to say to both of them. She remembered she had things to say to Reynolds, things she had fantasized getting the opportunity to say.

She heard a noise and sat up. Her head was fuzzy and she wondered if she had fallen asleep for a moment. It had been a breaking sound, glass. Right then it occurred to her she had a practical stranger in the house, an alcoholic; she was alone, he had a bottle of vodka, and he was angry.

Another noise followed and this one sounded like a thump and then something breaking. More crashing followed.

"What's going on?" she asked feebly. She made to get off the bed, then hesitated.

More banging and breaking. He was throwing a temper tantrum. Reynolds had never done anything like that before. Her Reynolds was a quiet and contained man. Mostly.

She tried to decide what to do but recognized fear was holding her there. That was her stuff being broken down there.

She scooted from the bed, opened the bedroom door, and hovered over the top of the steps. She heard a muffled voice, but it wasn't from the living room, which was right at the bottom of the stairs.

"Reynolds?" she asked. "What are you doing?" She ran down the stairs. He wasn't in the living room. The blanket and sheets were in a jumble. The bottle of alcohol was still on the table, the liquid inside at the same level as when she had set it there. The glass was next to it, but empty now. She picked up the bottle, holding it by its neck. Maybe she could try to ration it. She had a nasty vision of herself attempting to control him, get him to stay, through alcohol. She shook the idea away.

He's in the powder room and he's fallen down. She listened at the powder room door and then tapped with her index knuckle. "He-ay," she sang in a light voice.

"He-ay," she heard herself mimicked from behind.

She turned.

Doug Peel stood in her living room, holding her panties.

XXI. HUGGING

Doug Peel held the panties close to his face. He said, "I know what you're thinking. What the flying fuck are you doing here at this hour of the morning, right? But I don't want to hear it now, Dana."

Dana couldn't talk, couldn't move.

"Seems I'm gonna have to make a career out of saving you from bums and beggars." He breathed out loudly. "Are you okay?"

Dana managed to nod. She was trying to figure if he could cross the room before she opened the powder-room door, got in, and locked it. But it had one of those knobs that allowed a pin or a straightened paper clip to unlock it.

"C'mon over here. It's time we talked this out. I want us to be honest right from the jump. Okay?"

"Yes. Sure," Dana said. She had to get this guy out of the house before Franklin came home. She didn't want this nut anywhere around her boy.

She tightened her grip on the vodka bottle.

He looked back at the glass on the coffee table. "Drinking by yourself?" Then he saw the sheets. "He was sleeping here."

"Where is he?"

"You're picking up strays."

She wanted to hit him with the bottle and run out the front door to Brenda and Geoff's.

"I'm just trying to be a good citizen and do a good turn for somebody. You know, like you helped me out, right? Where is he?"

"Will you come here? Come on. Get these funky sheets off the couch and we'll talk. I'm not a loon, Dana. I know showing up like this is a gamble."

"Doug, why are you here?"

"Why—" He looked flustered then, his scary confidence broken.

Dana wanted to shout for Reynolds. If this crazy had hurt him, she was going to scratch his eyes out. She was getting angry enough to be able to move. "Yes. Why?"

He didn't appear to have a weapon. He said, "I should just go. I'm trying to look out for you, but if you don't want me here…"

"Later might be better, Doug. I'm not even dressed."

Dana stepped to her front door. *Get him out. Lock the door. Call Brenda and have her keep Franklin. Call the cops. Find Reynolds.* Her hand touched the front doorknob.

"Stop."

She didn't stop. She flipped the dead bolt, slid the chain.

"Stop."

"Let's go," she said. There was a trembling fear in her voice. She swallowed to try to lose it. "Come back later in the day. If you're nice, I'll fix you brunch." The door was a quarter of the way open. Should she run through it herself or wait to see if he would leave? Reynolds might need her.

"Do you like omelets, Doug? I make tasty—"

He leapt to her, covering the distance in two bounds. He slammed the door and slammed her against it. "I said, *stop*, hard-headed."

He pressed himself against her.

Dana raised the vodka bottle, but he caught her hand. He pinned it against the door and slowly slid it back down to her side.

"Hold still. Hold still."

He rubbed himself against her. He tried to kiss her, but she turned her face away. He kissed her ear while grinding his pelvis. He sucked air through his teeth, the sound of it right in her ear so that she felt it as well as heard it. It went on for several minutes with him gradually increasing the pressure the entire time. He was crushing her. She could hardly breathe. He moaned. His breath came in hot gusts against her cheek and neck. The skin over her left hip bone was pinched until she thought her bone must be tearing through. Dana's tears flowed. His guttural gasps burped over her face.

He stopped abruptly. He stepped back, trying to catch his breath. Their eyes met, his evaluating from under his bangs; he looked embarrassed. He took the bottle from her. He whispered, "You can get me off with just a hug, girl."

Tears dripped off her chin. "God damn it," Dana said, bent over and rubbing her hip bone.

"Well…you still haven't explained these." And he shook her panties in her face.

"You said you were going."

"I don't think I should leave until everything is understood. I don't want to mess this up."

"I have to use the bathroom."

A damp irregular square stamped the crotch of Peel's pants.

"I have to use the bathroom," she said again and moved toward the powder room.

He stepped in front of her, but she went around and into the room. She shut the door, locked it, for all the good that would do, and turned on the light. She covered her nose and mouth and gazed at her own wide eyes. What had that shit done with Reynolds? She recalled the pounding Peel had given Goat Man. Reynolds could be beaten or stabbed and bleeding out. He was either at the kitchen back door or in the basement if he was still in the house. She couldn't just stay in the powder room, though a large part of her urged her to put her feet to the door and never go out. How had Peel gotten in the house? Sitting on her patio smoking, he'd had time to figure that out, she supposed. She had to see about Reynolds and get this monster out before Franklin came home.

She turned on the water and splashed her face. She used the bottom of her pajama top to dry herself. The tears kept running.

She heard, "I'll leave when things are straightened out. And I can come back for brunch?"

Stop crying, she told herself. Look good; look calm. She took a breath. "Well, if you're coming back for brunch, maybe around ten, ten-thirty? We can talk it out then?" She checked the doorknob lock, then quickly pushed down her pants to inspect her hips and privates. They were just red. She wished she was wearing jeans and boots and a bra and a sweater. She wished she had her pepper spray. She checked under the sink. There was a rag and a can of Glade Floral Bouquet air freshener. Maybe if she sprayed him right in the eyes?

The bathroom doorknob wriggled as if of its own volition. It startled her. Peel had not answered her questions. Dana knew it was time to go back out there. For Reynolds and Franklin, for her family. "Coming," she sang. But another minute passed. The knob wriggled again more demandingly. "Okay," she said with more anger than she had wanted to reveal. "Right there." She took another deep breath, exhaled deliberately.

She opened the door.

———————

Peel still had the panties, but she couldn't see the vodka bottle anywhere. He gave her a big smile that made her shiver.

"Hey," she said softly and patted his arm.

She walked by him into the living room, looking around for Reynolds without being obvious about it.

Peel tagged right behind her.

She turned on the floor lamp by the couch.

Peel seemed to be examining the sheets. His lips tightened. She looked herself to see what he might be able to deduce.

"Do you want to go clean up?" she said in a low voice; she hoped it sounded offhand.

Peel looked at his stain. "Starch," he giggled. "Embarrassing." He gave a mischievous smile. "It'll dry."

"You haven't told me what you do for a living, Doug."

The sick smile gone, he eyed her with plain suspicion. The expression flipped into an open, amicable face. "Well, that's…it's not what somebody does for a living that tells you anything about them. It's what they wanted to do for a living. I worked for a large government intelligence agency." He nodded. "Oh, yeah. I'm the chief accountant. Well, was. I'm on disability right now."

"Disability? You? You seem in great shape."

"I wanted to coach. Pull these sheets off. They have homeless cooties." He laughed.

She pulled away the sheets, balling them up. Reynolds's clothes were beside the couch. No, the pants were not here. She placed the ball of sheets on top of Reynolds's things.

"I wanted to coach," he said again.

"Oh? What sport did you coach?"

"You're not listening, Dana." He shot a finger out to poke her, but she stepped away from it. He chuckled. "I said I wanted to. Football, the man's game."

"You played?"

"Yep. Well, I was on the team. I managed the equipment. I was always around the guys and the coaches…strength trainers. See, we're similar. You're a teacher and I wanted to coach, which is a glorified teacher, really."

She wanted to find Reynolds. "Can I get you something to drink? I have orange juice and sweet tea." She didn't wait for an answer but went quickly to the kitchen. She thought about the cutlery drawer.

But he stayed right on her heels as if he had thought about the knife drawer too.

Reynolds was not in the kitchen. Did he go for help? The back door was shut and locked. He might not go to the cops because he was afraid he was wanted. Or had he made that up?

"Juice?" She opened the refrigerator.

"No, no, no." He grabbed her wrist, shot her a look when she tried to pull it away. He led her back to the living room and to the couch. "Sit, please."

Dana sat and Doug Peel sat close to her.

He took a loud, dramatic breath. "Now, first, these," he said holding up her panties. "Tell me you didn't. Please. I mean I know you wouldn't let…" His voice cracked. He sniffed. "You wouldn't let that piece of human garbage get on top of you." He laid a hand on her upper thigh.

She immediately moved her leg and pushed his hand away. "Don't do that, Doug."

His facial expression didn't register her rebuke. It was as if she had said and done nothing.

"I took a load of dirty laundry to the basement earlier today. They must have fallen off the pile."

"That's it?"

"That's it."

He looked relieved. "I thought the worst, Dana." He smiled. "I thought he'd taken these off of you. I thought he had pulled these down your legs."

She reached for the underwear, but he held on to his souvenir.

"I didn't see any dirty clothes in the basement," he said, immediately suspicious again.

The basement.

"Washed, dried, and put away."

"And you missed these on each trip down there?"

"Yeah. Guess so. Where'd you find them, on the basement steps?"

The mannequin face returned. "He looks different than the guy you let in here."

Dana cast about for a weapon. There was nothing she could use within reach. Talking wasn't going to work.

"Answer the goddamned question!" His face bumped the side of her head.

She leaned away, holding a hand up defensively. "What question?!"

"He looks different than when he came in. Is it the same guy? The same one?"

"Oh, I…I loaned him my clippers. He shaved. Yes, he's the same guy. Same guy."

171

"Is the boy home? He's sleeping next door again, huh?"

Dana pictured in her mind what she should do.

"I know I'm being forward here. Mom would say, be a gentleman. I know we haven't known each other long, that we were just at the start. Not real dates, just micro-dates: joking in the grocery store...a long walk downtown...but..."

"But, what Doug?"

"It was a start, you know. I've seen you out walking. I've seen you searching. You walk like I do. Looking around the next corner before you ever get there. I know the world seems out of control, impossibly huge. And you want the thing that will bring it down to manageable size. So you look and look without really knowing you're doing it. And you think, I'm going to find the person, place, or thing that's going to make this whole spinning mess make sense."

He went on talking like that, but Dana didn't hear him. She saw light at her windows, the very first hint of morning. Brenda's household rose early. Brenda would offer Franklin breakfast, but he almost always declined, wanting to be home so he could nibble on a breakfast bar with his mom. It wouldn't be long until he was here.

Doug had asked her a question. She had only caught the last inflection in his voice and saw expectation on his face.

"I—I..." What did he want to hear? "It was a start to something for me too."

"Don't stall." Muscles from his cheek to his jaw twitched.

"I'm not."

"Did you cheat on our relationship? Did you cheat on me?"

In a fleeting blink, Reynolds grips the wheel but looks at Dana. She sees the hurt. She sees what she has done.

"No! I haven't."

Doug Peel looks unconvinced.

"Doug. I haven't cheated on you. I promise." She patted his hand.

He looked at her through slitted eyes. He was debating what he wanted to believe. He looked at the panties that argued counterpoint to Dana. The bangs covering his forehead made him look like a malevolent boy.

"We have so much to learn about each other."

"Yes."

He reached for her and pulled her to him. She did not resist. One hand went under her pajama top, inching up her back. She pushed toward him until he started sliding back.

"Hey. Hold on," he said.

She put a hand to his chest and pushed him all the way to his back. "What's wrong?"

"We have to get that freeloader out of your house."

She let her hair brush his face. "Doug, we found each other."

There was a bump and the jangle of keys.

Dana knew the source immediately, but Doug Peel looked toward the basement door. He tried to rise. As he brought his head up, Dana swung her elbow down with all the strength and weight she could muster behind it. It was a stunning collision that sent shockwaves up her arm. Peel fell back. Dana jumped off of him and hurdled over the coffee table just as Franklin was coming through the front door. "Franklin, get out of here. He's here! Call 911! Go to Brenda's and call 911!"

Her head was jerked back. Peel had a fist-hold of her hair.

Franklin froze.

"C'mere, kid," Peel shouted. "I don't want to hurt anybody."

"Go!" Dana screamed.

Dana was able to give him a shove out the door before being tugged back. She pushed off with her feet, adding her own momentum to the backward pull, and collided with Doug Peel. They fell to the floor. Peel lost his grip on her hair. Both jumped up. Peel lunged to the front door and slammed it shut. Dana scrambled to the basement. "The police are going to be on their way now. You'd better leave."

Dana opened the basement door and slammed it shut after her. It had no lock. Her hands reached for the light switch, but in her own house, even though she'd flicked the switch a thousand times without looking, she couldn't locate it, and ran down the stairs into the darkness. She almost tripped halfway down the staircase. Her hands grabbed the handrail and she managed to hold herself up.

It was Reynolds.

Her hands flitted over him. "Honey," she said.

"I'm here." His voice was shallow, full of effort. "Go out the basement window, quick. Get help. Go. I'll hold him here when he comes by."

"No, get up, let's both go."

The basement door burst open.

Doug Peel growled and leaped down the stairs.

Dana ran toward the lesser dark, a rectangular blue patch, the open window. It was chilly down here. Her bare foot kicked window glass on the floor. Somehow it was all in one piece.

She heard a crash behind her, a series of heavy thumps. Peel was shouting and cursing.

Dana jumped and got an elbow on the window's ledge. The cold morning air was on her face. She gasped, pulling herself up. How had Peel wormed his way through this opening? She heard grunting behind her. She heard Reynolds, the man she now knew to be her long-lost husband. There had been that moment when she doubted, just after she had shaved him, when the ten years of aging and abusive street life and facial injury had disguised him, when she let his own fear-wrapped denials sway her into wanting to go along with his charade, to avoid the pain and hassle she could see in his eyes. But it was a brief moment of weakness and she was not going to fault herself and she damn well wasn't going to leave her husband now that she had found him.

She worked her shoulders back through the window frame and dropped to the basement floor. One foot landed on something rigid and her ankle turned. The pain shot through her. She reached for the thing she landed on. It was a tire iron. From Peel's car, she guessed, and it was damp with blood. There was blood on the floor here too.

The two men were entangled at the bottom of the steps. Reynolds had Peel in a neck hold and Peel was struggling to free himself.

Reynolds was choking Peel. Peel could no longer make any sounds. He thrashed ineffectually.

Her eyes now adapted to the basement darkness, Dana could see the wide-eyed terror on Peel's face and the snarling determination on Reynolds's. She could see his blood too, flowing behind an ear. The muscles bulged on Reynolds's arm as it quivered and tightened. Peel was no longer moving.

"Reynolds," Dana said, but wasn't sure what she meant.

Reynolds's eyes met hers. He mouthed something and then his eyes rolled back. His arm went slack.

Peel sat up hacking and gasping, rubbing his throat. He swung a fist behind him, striking Reynolds, but Reynolds was already unconscious.

Peel fought to pull breath through his constricted throat. He looked up under his dangling hair at Dana. He needed just another moment. He was gathering himself. In his twisted mind he had probably saved her again from another homeless bum. They could talk this out. Maybe if they "hugged" again as they had done at the front door.

She did not want to walk as Peel walked, looking around corners before she came to them. Dana swung the tire iron. She swung it again. The feeling of the impact was horrible; the iron staved his skull and the sinking, the give of his skull, traveled up her arms.

She heard the iron clank on the basement's concrete floor. Peel flopped over. His arms hung awkwardly and he did not move or even twitch. He was partially on Reynolds. Dana grabbed Peel by the shirt and belt and managed to drag him off.

She found the light switch and flicked it on. That seemed to flick on the sirens too and their high pitch screamed nearer, swelling through the open basement window.

She kneeled between the two men, leaning over the man she called Reynolds. "Hey! Hey!" she said sharply.

His eyes fluttered. His tongue came out and licked his lips. "I choked him."

"Yes. And I hit him."

"Your stalker? The guy who hit me with his car?"

Dana nodded.

"And how's my stalker? She okay?"

"Yes. Fine."

"Good."

She hugged him, but not tightly. "You stay awake. Don't doze. I'm going to find Franklin; he must be frantic. Let him know Mom's okay."

She made it a point not to look at the body next to her. Halfway up the stairs, she looked back at Reynolds. His eyes were open. With one hand, he was testing the wound at the back of his head. "I'll get you some water," she said. "I'll be back in a moment."

———————

Policemen with drawn guns were coming up her walkway. Though she was prepared to see them, they still startled her.

"It's me. I live here. It's okay, I think," Dana shouted. She raised her hands. She knew from TV cop shows it was important to quickly identify yourself. She cast about for her boy.

Brenda had her hands on Franklin's shoulders and they stood at the bottom of the neighbors' steps. Nicole, Brenda's girl, had Franklin's hand. Geoff was talking to an officer. Four police cars were in front of Dana's house.

Franklin and Dana ran toward each other and collided in the front yard. Dana fell to one knee on the cold, crisp grass. They were both crying.

"Ma'am, is the intruder still on the premises? Ma'am?" A cop stood over them with his gun held at the side of his face pointing skyward.

"At the bottom of the basement stairs," Dana told him. "There's two men there. I'd better come with you."

"No, ma'am, you stay here. In fact, I need for you both to get back."

"The intruder is the white male fully clothed. The African-American man is my—" She was aware of Franklin listening through his sniffling. "...my house guest. He helped me."

He signaled with his free hand for them to stay put and joined the other officers. With his pistol looking like an extension of his nose, one jumped into the house first and the others rapidly followed.

Brenda and Geoff nearly dragged Franklin and Dana away. Everyone hugged her.

"We were so scared," Brenda said. "Are you...okay?"

Dana nodded.

"You have got to be cold."

"Pajamas and barefoot! I'm freezing." And she was just then aware of how cold she was.

Geoff said, "Let's wait inside. C'mon. It's safer."

"Oh, there's no danger. Peel's dead. He's dead. Pretty sure."

"Oh, Dana."

"I want to wait here."

An officer appeared in Dana's doorway. He signaled for Dana. "Ma'am, there's only one male at the bottom of the basement staircase."

XXII. REVISIONIST HISTORY

"He ran away as a little boy." This comes out of the blue, because the three of them have been sitting in uncomfortable silence for at least an entire minute.

"He ran away as a little boy," Maureen says.

"Mama." This from Ness, who probably prefers the silence.

Dana wishes they hadn't come. But they are holding true to Maureen's promise to "look in on her" until the baby comes.

They are arranged around Dana's living room. Maureen gets up, goes to the side table with the photographs, and picks up the wedding picture. Her eyes glisten.

Ness and Dana look at each other. At least they share this, a tiny, common dread at what comes next.

"Wasn't that a happy day," Maureen says. She doesn't look back at either of them for confirmation. "You two made such a handsome couple, just gorgeous. That's why I know the baby is going to be a beauty. Ness, you went with him to get the suit, didn't you?"

"No."

"I thought you did."

"No."

"Everyone feared it was going to rain. I knew it wouldn't. I said, didn't I? Didn't I say it wasn't going to rain?"

Another shared glance with Ness. "Yes, Mrs. Reynolds, I believe you did."

"First time he ran off was because he didn't get what he wanted for Christmas."

"No, it was because you didn't get him a guitar."

"That's what I said."

"An old used guitar from the pawn shop. Cheaper than what you gave him. He ran away 'cause…forget it."

Dana says, "Tell me." She wants Ness to speak, not Maureen.

"He weren't gonna play no guitar," Maureen says. She's still looking at the wedding picture.

"I'll tell you," Ness says to Dana. "He was frustrated that Mama didn't listen to him about the guitar. That's why," Ness talks in a slightly lower voice as if Maureen can't hear it.

Maureen says, "He was disappointed. He stayed away long enough for me to get worried, I'll tell you that. Sure did. How old was he then, Nessie? The first time."

Maureen picks up a photo Reynolds took of Dana. It was shot on Dana's birthday. She returns it.

"I don't know. Ten?"

"And the second time, he was in high school and he picked up with some new friends, hoodlum friends if you ask me."

"They weren't hoodlums, Mama."

"They were some sloppy looking, don't-care-about-a-damn-thing-looking boys. And I didn't want him hanging out with them, uh-uh. Where did he find them?"

"High school. They let anybody attend."

Dana smiles.

Maureen begins talking about the second time her son ran away from home. Dana isn't giving her full attention. She thinks of Ness, wondering why she has always wanted to be Ness's friend, why she's always a little sycophantic around Ness, even though the friendship never happens.

Ness doesn't think Dana is good for Reynolds, was good for Reynolds. She never did; Dana is sure of it. She was never fair with Dana. Dana has resented her for it and tried to win her over, practically wooed her at times. Stupid. Dana tells herself she doesn't care now, and mostly believes it. She shifts her legs trying to find a comfortable position, because all comfortable positions these days are fleeting. And now she is, probably, tied to these two women for the rest of their lives.

"So by the third day, I called the police back," Maureen is saying. She returns to her seat. Dana glances at the woman's face and realizes she has been caught not listening.

She feels like one of her kids caught talking to a neighbor during lecture time. "So what did the police do?" Dana asks.

"If it'd been a little white girl, they'd put out an Amber Alert and mobilize the reserves." Ness dares an argument from Dana.

"That's the truth," Dana says and regrets it. Sycophant.

"I don't think they had Amber Alerts back then."

"You're right, Mama."

"Well, anyway, he came back that evening in time for supper, but I hadn't fixed anything. He was a hungry and tired-looking boy. Too big to spank by then." Maureen looks away from the two younger women. "Never more happy to see him, though. Never more happy."

179

———————————

The police were still questioning Dana on her living room couch when the firemen and EMTs navigated the board with Doug Peel strapped to it up the basement steps and through the basement doorway. They kept her here when all she had wanted to do was to go down to the basement and see for herself. She told the entire story as truthfully as she could except for the identity of Reynolds, whom she called William, professing no idea of his last name. He was a man down on his luck whom she had befriended. *He needed a haircut and a meal. I made up the couch for him.* She pointed to the balled-up sheets and blankets Peel had made her remove. If he had crawled through that basement door and ran in his condition, barefoot, wearing just a T-shirt and pants, then he wasn't ready to face up to the authorities.

They laid Doug Peel on her living room floor. There was a plastic mask over his mouth and nose giving him oxygen. There were cold compresses around his head. He wore a collar. His shirt was open. He was very muscular and had sparse but long wisps of hair on his chest. They applied sensors to his chest.

"I'm just trying to get him there," one EMT said to another.

Don't work too hard, Dana thought. She couldn't believe he was alive; her hands and arms could still recall the sensation of impact from when she struck him. She told the men, the room full of men, what Peel had done to her at the door. That he had crushed her against it and had gotten off on it. The evidence of that could be found in his pants. They said they would bag his clothing. The tire iron came up in a plastic bag. Reynolds's fingerprints would not be on it, but his blood was. Both men's blood, and Dana's fingerprints, and maybe Peel's.

They lifted Peel to a gurney. In seconds, he was gone.

"It looks like he put duct tape on the window and then broke it out."

"Are you going to arrest me?"

"It looks funny, Mrs. Reynolds. That your friend ran. He was your corroboration. Is he in trouble that you know of?"

Dana shook her head. "No. No, he's just afraid of, you know, you guys, authority. He had no reason to leave."

"Ma'am, when you hit the intruder with the tire iron, were you in imminent danger? Did you fear for your life?" The policeman's eyes bore down on Dana.

"You feared for your life, ma'am?" the other one asked.

"Yes, yes. He was pissed. He was coming after me. I thought he would kill me and William. I filed a report on him before."

"Okay. He was physically coming toward you?"

Dana adjusted the memory of Peel trying to catch his breath. She changed it for all time and all retellings. Now, he was coming to his feet, reaching out to her. She said, "Yes." Tears rolled down her face. They handed her a paper towel from her kitchen. "I want to see my son."

Mother and son sat on her bed while activity continued below them. After the officers, she had spoken to a few detectives, saying the same thing. It was a test. She thought she passed. The story she gave Franklin, eager to hear that all was okay, was the same she'd given the detectives, except for the assault at the front door. "He wanted to kiss me," she told him, "and got mad when I wouldn't let him."

When the last officer was leaving, she asked after Peel's condition. The latest word he had gotten was that Peel was in a coma.

Dana and Franklin napped together for the first time in four or five years. Dana heard a knock at the door, a rapid, urgent knock, and thought it could only be Brenda, who had brought over food earlier.

Halfway down the stairs she heard a yelp. It came from the back, and she hurried to the kitchen door. When she became aware Franklin had followed her, she told him to go back upstairs.

He stayed behind her.

Reynolds was at the kitchen door, a pained expression on his face.

Dana opened the door as quickly as she could, fumbling with the locks.

"Get in here! Where'd you go?"

"My feet are numb! I sat on tacks!"

"It worked!" Franklin shouted. "Wrong guy though. Hi, William."

"Hi, Franklin. They'd hurt worse if my ass wasn't frozen."

Franklin and Reynolds laughed. Reynolds eyed Franklin the entire time.

"Get blankets, Franklin. We'll soak your feet in warm water."

Reynolds went to the sink. He held up a finger and shook his head. He vomited into the sink. His entire body heaved. His back curled. "Sorry," he said. His body heaved again. He wiped his mouth, turned on the faucet, and let the water run. "I could use a drink."

"I don't know what Peel did with the bottle."

"Dana."

"I'll find it."

Twelve steps and soon, she told herself.

Her men were on the couch with the TV on.

"You know a lot about comic books."

"I used to collect."

Franklin nodded. Of course. He seemed to enjoy the presence, and the attention, of this "old family friend."

Dana was in the kitchen heating soup for Reynolds. She had discovered the vodka bottle where Peel had rolled it under the couch. She had given Reynolds one drink. He had looked at her when she walked away with the bottle.

"I thought you said you have all the *Thors*?"

"Well, my grandmother has them. She says they're mine, but she doesn't want to part with them yet because they were my dad's. It's the truth."

"I believe you," Reynolds said.

Dana detoured to the windows frequently. She was either looking for returning police or for Doug Peel, sitting in his car, waiting for her to venture outside.

When Reynolds's feet came out of the soak, he could wiggle his toes. He had hidden in the trees that stood between the town houses and a neighborhood of single-family houses. He raked leaves over himself and believed he managed to remain awake the entire time, listening for the cops he knew were coming.

Franklin said, "You must have been so cold."

"Not my first time."

Dana took a shower. She inspected her hip again for bruises. She scrubbed at her ear and neck where Peel had breathed and grunted on her.

Franklin burst in just as she was drying off.

"Franklin!" she said, but then saw his face. "What?"

"William's getting dressed. He says he has to leave."

Dana dressed quickly in jeans and a cable-knit sweater. Though in a hurry, she took a moment for one thing. She lifted the top tray of her jewelry box, found the band, and slipped it on.

Reynolds had his socks and shoes on, but was still on the couch. He saw her running down the stairs and looked away.

"What is going on?" Dana asked.

He smiled briefly, but still didn't look her way. "It wouldn't be good for me to stay. The police…"

"Don't give a damn about you, Rey—William. William. They have the true story, a true enough story, and all the evidence they need. I may need a lawyer. Damn it."

He shook his head.

She sat beside him. "Franklin, let the adults talk, please."

"I'm not stopping you. I'm just listening."

"Franklin," Reynolds said.

He turned and went upstairs, but was probably just out of sight on the top step.

Dana bumped her shoulder against Reynolds's. "Did I thank you for saving me from Peel? You did, you know."

"Well, if I did, it's the least I could do." He was looking at his hands that lay curled, palms up, in his lap. "For your real husband, who's maybe still out there somewhere, looking for a way to come home."

"Yeah?"

"Sure."

"Do you think he knows I love him? Love him horribly. And that I always have? Even when…even when I messed up."

"Well," he said. He wiped his eyes.

Dana whispered, "If he stays away now…it's not just me. He's staying away from his son too."

"He didn't know you were pregnant. Did he?"

"No. Your feet are in no condition for carrying you around."

"I can't stay here."

"You can. I want you to. We want you to."

He was either looking into the kitchen or at nothing at all. She was going to lose the battle. He wasn't going to stay.

"But I know another place you can stay." The idea just hit her.

He turned to her and she smiled at him, ready to sell her idea. "Out of town, no police. You'll be safe. We'll go by an ATM; I'll get you some money."

"Where?"

"There's an ATM right up the—"

"Where's this place?"

"Out of the area. Safe."

They packed a duffle with his clothes. Dana remembered she should put some toiletries in the bag. When she unzipped it, she saw a framed photo of her and Franklin at the zoo, taken that summer. He had removed it from the bookshelf. She put the vodka bottle in there too, though there wasn't much left.

"Franklin, can you be a big boy for your mom and stay here?"

"No."

"Go over to Brenda's if you feel uncomfortable."

"Going with you." He looked determined, and Dana had to admit she would not like being without him right now.

"Fine."

He stepped close. She thought he was going to hug her, but he asked, "Where are we going to take him?"

Dana put her lips to his ear. "To Grandma's."

XXIII. AND IS FOUND

He fell asleep. For that, Dana was grateful, because she did not know how he would have reacted if he saw they pointed south for Fredericksburg.

"How long does a coma usually last? On average," Franklin asked from the back seat.

"Hmm, that's a good question. We may have to Google that. But, honey, we don't have anything to worry about, because even if he did wake up, they'd just escort him off to jail."

"Yeah," Franklin sounded unconvinced.

Dana peeked at her son in her center rear view. She could see so much of Reynolds in him now, more and more as he grew older. He had such a pretty skin color. He put his earphones in. He stared out the window, his light brown eyes glinting. He looked so thoughtful.

Except for soft snoring from Reynolds, it was a quiet ride. Just before they left, she had remembered to call a substitute for her class and to call in sick for Franklin.

They were in Fredericksburg, very near his old neighborhood, when Reynolds began to stir.

Dana whispered, "Crap."

He sniffed, sat up, and looked about. "Where are we?"

She ignored the question the first time. They waited at a light. When he asked again she said, "Close."

"This is…no. Hell no."

"William," she emphasized the name as a way of reminding him Franklin was in the back seat. "You'll be safe."

"This is just where I don't want to be. Where I can't be." His hand went to the door latch.

"The police won't think to look for you here."

"No. Stop the car."

"Two blocks more."

"Stop the damn car."

"Mom."

"Wait." Dana kept going.

Reynolds reached for the steering wheel.

The car jerked.

"Mom!"

"Okay, okay! Damn." Dana pulled over.

"Hand me the bag, Franklin," Reynolds said. He opened his door and stepped out.

"What's going on?" the boy asked.

"Hand me the bag, son."

Dana stopped at the word "son" from Reynolds. The man and boy seemed to take no special notice of it.

Franklin handed the bag between the seats. Reynolds snatched it and walked away.

"Stay here," she said and pushed the gearshift into park and turned on her flashers. She climbed out on the passenger side.

He walked so quickly, Dana had to jog to catch up.

She called "William" and then she called "Reynolds." He did not turn around. She stopped, watched him moving away. She shouted at the top of her lungs, "Will you please stop running away!"

He stopped. He turned and looked at her from nearly a block away.

She wondered what he was seeing right then. The woman standing with her arms crossed on the sidewalk, shivering a bit, was the woman he had married, not the fool he had left. Didn't he recognize that? He turned and walked away. *He doesn't love me anymore*, Dana thought. *And why should he?*

"She's sick!"

He stopped. He turned and started back towards her. Dana had time to think of what to say. Nothing adequate was occurring to her.

"Who's sick?" he asked, three yards away.

"Your mother."

"My mother—lady, I'm not your husband. That means whoever is not my mother."

"It's cancer." She saw the blow strike home; it was like taking the tire iron to Peel.

"You're delusional. You better be careful. You might end up out here with the rest of us." Now he was just two steps away.

"Reynolds…"

"Not Reynolds!"

"You gave yourself away," Dana chuckled. "Only Reynolds would know he was being taken home."

"I thought you were taking me to DC. I don't want to be out here in southern provincial!" Now he was in her face.

"Bullshit."

"You want your husband back. He's gone! Maybe he fell in the river. Maybe he wandered off and died. Either way. I'm sorry, but don't try to recreate him, Dana. There's no going backwards in this, this thing. There's no such thing as counter-clockwise. Move on. For the boy's sake, move on, and leave the worthless drunk alone."

"You owe me."

"What?"

"William owes me. Haircut, clothes, drinks…sex."

"Oh my God!"

"Reynolds owes me nothing, but William owes me big time."

"I can't believe you."

"You fooled me. I want you to fool her, too."

Franklin opened his door just before the car stopped in front of Maureen's. "William, I can show you all my comics now!" he said and dashed down the walk for the front door.

Reynolds may not have heard him; his focus seemed to be on the house. He said, "I don't know about this."

Dana saw Ness's car parked across the street.

"But she might not recognize me, right?"

"Right." What world was he in where a mother would not recognize her son? "Take your cue from Maureen. If she thinks you're Reynolds, play along. If not, I'll just say you're an old friend of Reynolds's and mine."

He nodded and still they sat there for quite a long time more. Dana thought of things to say and dismissed each one. Her Reynolds had never been this afraid.

Dana imagined: *He walks into the house. It has been a particularly trying morning. He has come home early just to get away from it all, or he forgot the spreadsheet he was working on and thought he'd dart home, retrieve it, and be back before he is missed. He wouldn't recognize Steve's car, parked on the street as it is. He sees her car and wonders. He puzzles over the back door being unlocked. Is his wife feeling ill? He is about to call out her name, maybe he takes in some air to shout her name, but for some reason—say she's ill and taking a nap—he wouldn't want to wake her. Concerned, he walks in quietly. His head is filled with ordinary thoughts: maybe Dana's allergies are hitting her, maybe there's time for me to run to the pharmacy for her.*

Thirsty, he opens the refrigerator, hoping there is chilled water, but again, whoever had the water bottle last did not refill it. He shakes his head and automatically blames Dana—you would think a teacher would be more responsible. He spots the milk carton, shrugs, and pulls it out. He pinches the spout open and sniffs it. There's no odor. He doesn't bother with a glass. He drinks a little, but then he hears a noise, voices maybe, or he hears a squeak or scrape; it's something minute and hushed. He forgets the carton as he sets it down. He puts the noise together with the unlocked door and thinks thieves. They have Dana's keys, took her car, and drove over to her address in the glove compartment to see what else they could get. So he moves quietly to surprise whoever he will find. Another sound directs him to the bedroom. Does he stand in the doorway for several seconds trying to reconcile what he sees, or does he turn away immediately? Is he stunned to immobility, or embarrassed and flees? Regardless, everything is changed, and he is the one surprised.

———————

Dana waited for him to make the first move, because she wasn't sure what to do next. She had begun to suspect that he was truly in denial about who he was. Maybe this was the right time to say the things she had dreamed of saying in all those years of second-chance fantasies.

He snapped the latch. "Let's go."

She smiled and nodded, but he didn't see her. He was climbing out of the car.

Dana jogged around the car to catch up with him. "She's in chemotherapy," she said.

Maybe he nodded.

"It's tough on her."

The door was still partially opened. Franklin appeared. "It wasn't locked," he said. "C'mon."

It was warm inside, stuffy. No one was in the front room. Dana feared Ness's appearance, not knowing how Reynolds would react. One thing at a time. She watched Reynolds look around.

"Stop that," he said to her.

"What?" she asked even though she knew what. "They've made her a bedroom in the dining room." Dana followed Franklin down the hall. She looked back, fearing Reynolds would run. He was motionless, but she could see him continuing to struggle with his demons, the ones that had perched on his shoulder and rode his back for nearly ten years, whispering to him that he could not go home. She thought of going back and taking his hand, but he needed to punch these demons himself. Let him win this one on his own.

She heard Franklin and Maureen, but not Ness.

She expected to find Maureen bedridden, but she was standing in the middle of her kitchen, hugging her grandson with a warm smile on her face. An aluminum walker was next to them. There was no sign of Ness.

"Hello, Dana," Maureen said. "Thanks for my surprise."

"I'm glad you like surprises," Dana said.

Down the hallway, the real surprise had taken two steps forward, near the foot of the staircase, and froze again.

Dana was afraid to take her eyes off him. If he ran this time, if he ran one more time, she knew he would be gone forever. She signaled him to come forward, but wasn't sure he saw her. She walked over to Maureen and the women hugged.

"You're looking so much better!"

"Oh, I got a little bit of energy left. At least for part of the day. They eased off on my dosage."

"You look great, Grandma! Why, you're probably strong enough to bake a cake."

"Franklin!"

"Well…"

Dana lowered her voice, "Is Ness here?"

"She's rummaging through the closets upstairs. Says she left some shoes over here."

"Grandma, wait till you hear what happened to Mom."

"No. We are not going to bother her with that now. You know, a lot of stuff is coming out of your mouth. Go to your aunt, help her find her shoes. Go on." Dana was grateful for an excuse to send him from the room.

"I'll be right back," he said.

Dana peeked down the hall. Franklin passed Reynolds. Her son said something, but Reynolds did not reply. Franklin's flying leaps thumped on the stairs.

Maureen gripped the walker as soon as Franklin left. Her hands were knuckled to it and her arms trembled. Dana wrapped an arm about her and tried to take some of the weight.

"Thank you, daughter," Maureen said.

Maureen had never called her that before.

"I want you to tell me the latest about Warren. Have you seen him again? How is he getting on?"

Dana swallowed. "Do you want to sit down?"

"I think I'd better."

Maureen's weight suddenly increased and Dana, awkwardly positioned, struggled to keep her from falling. The walker was in the way, but Maureen clutched it tightly. "We need some help in here," Dana said. She kept her voice level. "Some help."

And then he was there. Right beside the two women. He took Maureen by the waist and by an elbow. Dana transferred the weight to him.

She pulled out a chair from the kitchen table. "Or do you want to get back in bed?"

"No, this is fine." Maureen said to Reynolds, "Thank you, honey. Such a gentleman."

"You're welcome," he said.

"Dana, introduce me to your handy friend. I'm Maureen Reynolds."

"Um." No words would come. Dana looked from the man she called Reynolds to Maureen. *Handy friend.* Now it was Dana who wanted to run. She thought she would too, if Franklin had not been upstairs.

Maureen looked from Dana to the man leaning over her. Dana caught the moment her mother-in-law first truly saw the man who had eased her into the chair. She saw the eyes grow and glisten, the lips tremble. "Warren!" Maureen said, but it came out muffled because she had already launched herself into him, her face buried into his chest.

His arms encircled her. "I'm sorry, Mama. I'm sorry, please."
"Before God. Before God."
"Mama."
"And is found," Maureen said.
Dana made no move to wipe her wet face.
Ness was there with a pair of pumps. "I told you I left these here. With your big feet, I know you didn't think they...what's... no. No!" The shoes dropped to the floor.
And then it was the three of them, enwrapped tightly, melded, shapeless, crying, sometimes in danger of teetering over.
Dana put a hand over her mouth, watching them until the scene blurred.
It was Ness who reached out and grabbed Dana's arm. "You found him," she said, and pulled Dana, with surprising force, into the circle.

XXIV. WHAT HAD MRS. LAZARUS SAID?

The screen door opened the moment she placed a foot on the porch. He may have been watching her the entire time she had been parking the car and walking slowly up the sidewalk. She had been distracted by a large flock of birds squawking in the giant oaks across the street. The flock was so huge that the nearly bare trees appeared full again, but with black, animated leaves.

"Those birds," she said as he opened the door, but couldn't think of anything to remark about them.

He mumbled something and stepped out rather than letting her in.

It was chilly outside and the sky was a pale, uncommitted color.

He wore only a T-shirt. He did not touch her, but stepped aside and sat on the top porch step.

Her hand had lightly brushed his arm as he went by. She looked down at him sitting there. His hair was just beginning to thin in back. "Chilly out here," she said.

He didn't reply.

She buttoned her coat and joined him on the step.

He scooted over to put a few inches of space between them.

"Franklin didn't come," he said. He was looking at the dismal front yard.

"He will on the weekend. Homework." She added, "He's coming around. Asking a lot of questions that I don't know the answers to. But I tell him the answers I do know, Reynolds, even if they are embarrassing; I tell him."

He breathed out loudly and the breeze took the mist from his face.

"Ness said the other day you said something about pulling up stakes."

"She takes off from work just to watch me."

"Ness is worried—"

"Ness is scared."

Dana spotted her sister-in-law's car parked down the street.

"Well, are you?" And she looked at his face, his profile, chin studded with short pins of hair, vapor issuing from his broad nose. She swallowed. "Are you going to run again?"

He shrugged. "I think about it every day." His hands went up in some incomplete gesture, in front of a half-formed thought. He said, "I have you all fooled now." He looked at her briefly. "Into thinking I'm this Reynolds of yours."

"Yeah, I guess so. The thing is, *Reynolds,*" she emphasized the name, "if you worked at it, you could fool yourself too."

"Hah."

"Don't laugh."

"This Reynolds must have been quite a guy."

"He was," she said quickly.

He chuckled.

"No, he was." Her hand lit on his knee. "He meant everything to me." She took a breath. "And I haven't been much without him."

"Until he was swept down the river and out to sea."

"Don't."

"Well, if he meant so much, why did you…why did you play out on him?"

Dana took her hand away. She had practiced this, in her mind, finding the words to ask for his forgiveness. In those rehearsal vignettes, she had been the one to bring it up. *Reynolds, I want to tell you how sorry, how very sorry I am.* "That's what I've been wanting to tell you for a while now." She sniffed. "For years…"

And suddenly all those years seemed to be wedged between them in the inches of space separating her hip from his, her knee from his, like a force field, making him not the man she had so long dreamed of, but a stranger, and making her a fool for thinking it could be some other way.

The door opened behind them. "Oh, there you are," Ness said.

He said, "Here I am."

"Hey, Dana."

Dana turned. Ness was holding the new brown coat Dana had bought Reynolds. "Hey, Ness. How's Mom today?"

"She's good. She's okay. We go for chemo in a few minutes or so. Warren, your coat."

He didn't look back. "I'm good."

"It's cold out here."

"I'm good."

"That's what your problem is." Dana detected a note of humor in her sister-in-law's voice.

"What's my problem this time, Your High Ness?"

"You don't know when to come in from the cold." Ness laughed.

Dana pressed her lips together for a look between smiling and not smiling. She looked to Reynolds and wasn't sure if he'd smiled or not.

"Now that Dana's here you don't have to go to the hospital with us. And she can take you on to your meeting."

"I want to go with you and Mom."

"We just sit around. I don't want you to miss your meeting."

"I won't. I can walk from there, if her treatments run long."

"Dana, get him to put his coat on." Ness tossed it to Dana, who leaned back to catch it.

She stepped back in the shadow of the house and the door shut.

Dana did not try to get him to put his coat on. Instead she wrapped the coat across her legs. She felt instantly warmer. "Cozy," she said and rested her crossed arms on her legs. Moments went by with neither of them moving. It was time to say what needed to be said. Dana felt the inside of her throat thicken. She opened her mouth, but only vapor wisps came out. She squeezed her hands together in her lap. "Reynolds," she said and this time he faced her. "Reynolds, when I thought you were dead, it tore me up that I didn't get the chance to apologize, to explain. And I tried to find reasons for what I did, but stupid...stupid is hard to explain. It wasn't because of you in any way...what I did. You just married somebody who still had this selfish...oh. Damn. Warren Reynolds, I'm sorry."

Reynolds stood and went down the walk a few steps. His back was toward her. She didn't know if she should stand up too.

"You already apologized that night."

"Did I?"

"In the car."

"Oh. That woman was just trying to get out of trouble."

He turned. The morning light caught the tear tracks on his face. "You apologizing...I'm the one needing redemption. Don't think I don't know it. It's just...maybe Reynolds did die. I have a lot to make up for. To Franklin, to Mom and Ness, and most of all to you."

Dana stood, holding his coat against her.

"I just don't know if I can do it. I want to run. There's this antsy, crawling feeling comes over me. I get scared. My job wasn't going well. My marriage wasn't going well. And scared is just as hard to explain as stupid."

Dana walked to him and put her forehead on his chest. She wanted to ask him not to run away again. "Please," she began, nearly inaudible. She didn't know if he had heard. But then she sensed he might view what she said as pressuring him, so she said nothing more. What she wanted to say was that if he would just hold on to her and Franklin, and Mom and Ness, they would purge all the crawly and antsy from him and he wouldn't have to be scared again. *I know men get scared sometimes, Reynolds, it's all right.* She would say that to him too.

She waited. She would wait.

And after a long moment, his arms came up and encircled her there in the front yard, on the sidewalk.

He lies on the top portion of his father's old bed. He's on his side in a slight curl. She has the drop on him and watches him for a full minute before he realizes she's at the doorway. He has his earphones in, which explains why he had not investigated the shrieking from the floor below, and a spread of comic books in front of him. The resemblance to his father seems more pronounced than ever. In that room, surrounded by comics, he could have been Warren Reynolds from years ago.

"Hey," he says, finally noticing her. He pulls out an earplug.

She is still on that warm high from the reunion and she thinks, *What did Mrs. Lazarus say to her children?* She says, "Hey back to you. Didn't you hear all that hollering going on downstairs?" She steps into the room, sits on a sliver of bed where there are no comics.

"Yeah, I thought you guys were just joking or something. Is William coming up? I want to show him my collection. Have you been crying?"

"No. Well, yeah. For good reasons. Um, didn't you say there was a new *Captain America*? I want to read that one."

He looks at her suspiciously. "That's a new comic. These are Dad's old ones."

"Oh." Dana slides a comic toward her. It is in a plastic, custom-fit bag. He sees her puzzle over it, reaches over, and removes the comic from the bag for her. He returns to his reading.

Dana says, "You told me once Bucky Barnes is the new Captain America. But I thought Bucky died a long time ago."

Franklin looks up. "Yeah, well, no one ever really dies. They turn up again, sooner or later."

Dana says, "Funny you say that. I have really good news, but it's really strange news too. It's good, but it's…wild." She wings it, fearful of the psychology involved. Will this scar him?

Franklin takes the news quietly. But his boy's mind is turning it all over and over. For Franklin there was never a question that his father might not have been dead. Maureen had not burdened him with her hopes, so truly, his father was back from the grave, a feat only heroes like Captain America had pulled off. But he was more bashful around Reynolds now, staring at him when Reynolds wasn't aware. They had shaken hands, all very male, Dana thought, and Franklin had enjoyed that.

She has to tell him that his father's return needs to be a family secret for a while: "We don't want him to get in trouble for helping me with Peel." Plus there is the little matter of the insurance money to figure out.

He says, "He could have called. He could have called from a pay phone and just let you know he was alive. He could have called Grandma."

"Yes."

And late one evening he walks into the kitchen in his pajamas and says, "I don't know what to call him. I can't…I mean…Dad? Mr. Reynolds? Warren?"

Dana says, "What about just sir? Hello, sir. Excuse me, sir, pass the salt please."

"Sir." He tests it, nods, and goes back to bed.

———————

Dana pulled her car off to the side into the empty lot. She climbed out, telling Franklin to wait, but she heard the latch of his door release.

"Who are you looking for, Mom?"

"Hmm? Oh, just thought for a second…I thought it might be a friend of mine, someone who helped me out." She took a few steps from the car. She could not tell if the person she spotted had green high heels or not, could not tell whether it was female or not. Finally, the person slipped between two buildings. It looked more like the two buildings were converging on her as the alley narrowed in the distance. The figure was still within earshot, but Dana did not call out. She hated the idea of Jessie having to leave because of Doug Peel, because of her. Maybe Jessie had gone into DC, a more accommodating place in many ways for the homeless. She might have gone there where the panhandling was easier, and more expected, and she could better camouflage herself amongst its anonymous numbers. Dana thought she might try there, maybe on weekends, find an excuse for Franklin and her to go downtown to see a museum. But she could not conceive of when they would have time for such excursions. Chances were that the shrinking figure was not Jessie. And maybe that was a good thing, if it meant she had given up the streets. Maybe she'd gotten into a halfway house, established an address, and gotten a job, sailed through the between-space to earth once more.

Does that ever happen? Do the homeless ever work their way home? Or like Reynolds, do you have to reach out and pull them in? And would they stay if you did?

Movement and then sound distracted her skyward. A huge flock of small birds was sitting on the power lines that paralleled the street. The birds looked black against the sky, but they may have been any color. They occupied every inch of the cables, many sitting, many flapping with discontent or impatience. Suddenly, they lifted. As if by secret signal the flock took to the air, forming a pixilated cloud. It canted and suddenly changed direction.

"Do you think he's going to come live with us?" Franklin asked.

"That I do not know, honey," she answered. "Would you like that?"

The boy shrugged. "Do you want him to?"

"Yes."

The birds seemed to gather themselves. Strays were allowed to catch up, to rejoin the whole. She could hear not only their chaotic calling, but the powerful aggregate beating of their wings. She wondered at their brilliant, cohesive unanimity. Dana started at the touch of Franklin's hand sliding into hers. He had become a hand-holder and willing hugger lately, a by-product, Dana figured, of all he had witnessed, the new uncertainty of things that had revealed itself. But it would not last forever, these longer hugs and kisses on the cheek, so she accepted them gratefully while she could. She looked into her boy's eyes and saw Reynolds. Their eyes were an exact match, the shape and the color and the way he turned them on her too. She saw the man she had married, a distillation of him and her, a finer, truer, more hopeful version.

"Let's go," Franklin said, tightening his hold on her hand and gently tugging at her.

She looked up. Across the asphalt lot, damp and windswept, and empty on a weekend morning, the figure she had spotted had disappeared entirely.

"C'mon."

"Okay, Franklin," she said and let herself be led back to the car.

ABOUT THE AUTHOR

O.H. Bennett is the author of three earlier novels, *The Colored Garden*, *The Lie*, and *Creatures Here Below* (Agate Bolden, 2011). A graduate of the George Mason University writing program, he lives in Northern Virginia.